Through The Cracks

A miscellany of stories & parables

by

Bushra Naqi

Through The Cracks

ISBN 978-1-8-380893-9-9

Published in 2020
North Staffordshire Press
Smart Innovation Hub
Keele University
ST5 5NS

Bushra Naqi is a poet and short story writer based in Lahore, Pakistan. Over the course of her writing career, she has published three poetry books with this collection of short stories representing her first foray into short story writing. Her writings draw inspiration from her myriad of experiences living in Pakistan and portray both the vast canvas of its social milieu and the ambivalence of its social fabric.

Bushra is a recipient of the Patras Bokhari award by the State of Pakistan for her writings.

' I dedicate this book to my son, Fahad Shams, who worked alongside with me on the book.'

Table of Contents

A CANTALOUPE

'What does a cantaloupe mean, my princess?' asked the man as he sat at her feet, caressing their snow-white softness. The princess whom he addressed was a tall, middle-aged woman with short, curly black hair that circled around her long swan-like neck. She looked at him with an amused and loving glance, taking in his naiveté instantly. 'Love, it is a fruit from the melon family, deliciously sweet, like true love,' she replied in her lilting voice. Otherwise, she thought, he looked like a man of the world, with the confidence of one born in a society that put all men on a pedestal of privilege. Yet he sat there stroking her feet in humility that was born from self-assurance that was not easily rocked. He was a younger man, perhaps fifteen years younger than the princess, but neither were discomfited by this uneven equation. He was a tall man with a slightly rounded figure, which did not embarrass him at all. On his ruddy, round face a bushy moustache twirled like a bird's plumage. His brown eyes that shone with kindness were the best part of his face.

Later these two besotted souls fell into each other's arms like two thirsty wanderers, adrift but focused on one another, eye to eye and body to body.

Ever since the man and woman had met quite by chance at a musical evening, they had sought various ways to be together. That day was distinct in many ways. The skies had been sombre and ominous, with heavy rain. She had been queuing at the theatre when it began to rain and had rushed into the auditorium where the musical performance was being held. The woman, whom the man later nicknamed Princess, was dismayed to find that her lovely dress had been half soaked, when he appeared from behind her and sheltered her with his black umbrella. She thanked him with glowing eyes. There was something that she liked about him that she could not quite place. It was another coincidence that they later sat side by side in the huge auditorium. Throughout the evening an electric current flowed from one body going through to the other, with both acutely aware of the other's presence.

The audience was enthralled by renditions of the great classical singer Ustad Rehmat Ali, whose powerful body swayed rhythmically as his heavy-lidded eyes rolled with ecstasy. The woman applauded and in a soft voice called out 'Bravo!' and the man clapped his hands vigorously. The woman whispered, half turning to the man, 'The Ustad stirs my heart on a spiritual level. He turns the mundane into a spiritual experience.' His heart missed a beat as it dawned on him that she was a woman of great depth and intuition. She was exceptional! And in that moment he knew he wanted her. Suddenly the lights went on and he felt as if he was utterly naked in his thoughts. He blushed to the roots of his hair, relieved that no one was privy to his thoughts. As they were leaving the auditorium the man asked her casually, on impulse, 'What is your phone number? We really must meet again to continue our critique of the great Ustad.' The woman smiled a vague smile that lingered between her lips and eyes, nodding acquiescence. She gave him her number, still distracted, and bade him goodnight without looking back.

For many days the woman kept pondering over the chance

meeting with the stranger. It was brief but the impression was intense. She had been single for many years now; her divorce had shattered her but at the same time given her new life. It had been a loveless marriage, her husband had been a mature and sober man, much older than she was. A doctor by profession, he was so immersed in his work that he barely noticed her. This lovely young woman had kindled no lasting love in him. She felt used, abandoned and scorned by him, while her own withering contempt eroded any remnant of love he might have felt for her. Trapped in this marriage, they turned cold and callous towards each other. The child they bore suffocated under their strained relationship. As she coldly watched him, she was afraid their relationship might impact her life. He had little time for the innocent child, so great was his preoccupation with his work. She knew they had nothing to give to each other and lived like two solitary beings, straying further apart into their human shells. Divorce was the inevitable outcome. He resented it and did not want to let go of her, for she was his only connection to any intimate bonding. They parted with the same bitterness they had lived with for years, no more, no less.

She shuddered as she looked back on those days. Her adored daughter had been her only consolation. She was growing up to be beautiful, with no resemblance to her father, making it easier to erase him from her mind, like rubbing a slate clean. The child clung to her, and she knew it was not only from love. It was fear that was not easy to ignore. Time would heal her spirit, she would see to that. Everything healed in time, and life would be restored to normalcy.

Today a soft breeze lulled her as she recalled the stranger. She had not even asked his name. There was a thrill in someone being anonymous, like a shadowy image tantalizing the mind. Only that morning there had been a call. It was him. 'Can we meet today at Cafe Soz?' said a hoarse voice at the other end. She answered in her soft, lilting voice, 'I'll be happy to be there, I am happy you called.'

When she arrived at Cafe Soz, there were very few people sitting there as it was too late for lunch and early for dinner. The waiters were lounging, idle and bored, at the end of the room. He was sitting in the far corner, away from public view, from where he could see her enter. She was elegantly dressed in bold colours, and her face was done up modestly - perfect for the occasion. He felt elated as the picture he had painted of her in his mind was coming alive. 'Hi!' she said breathlessly, apologizing for being late. He rose. 'Hi!' he smiled sweetly and pulled out a chair for her. They were complete strangers to each other, but an electric current swept through them and pulled them together. They talked intimately, like two long lost friends who have a lot of catching up to do. They had no time to waste on frivolities.

He told her that he was married, caught in a loveless marriage. They were holding up, he and his wife, because they felt they did not have a choice. She clung to him because she feared being alone with their child. They were no longer lovers, merely acting out a role. Love and passion had long ago been washed away. Mundane matters had taken over their lives. They were like two lost souls and when the going got tough, she tightened the noose around his neck to make his escape impossible.

Initially, he said, they had been friends.

'It was only after we were married that her true nature was revealed and love sneaked out through the backdoor. Now we have become strangers to one another and all we do is hurt each other, nothing else. You know, when love fades away it mutates into hate.'

Quietly the woman took it all in with composure. It had been impossible to believe that he was a free man, yet she had hoped. But as he looked endearingly into her eyes, she knew that she did not care. A tidal wave had stormed into her life and now there was no holding back. She wanted to let destiny take its course. She was a believer in fate and had learned not to resist. She took his hand into hers, very trustingly and warmly. They conversed on every topic imaginable. He was an erudite man, though he did not look it. There was humility in his learning and no absolutes in his life. She believed in, 'I agree to disagree,' and their discourse was fulfilling in its richness of meaning and depth.

The man and woman continued to meet whenever the opportunity arose. In intimate moments they unlocked feelings that were dormant in both, and releasing them was breathing in fresh air. They were in reality two starved souls who were craving for love, and they nourished each other. Their passion was like a raging river rushing towards an unknown destination. Sometimes he would ask, 'Princess, tell me what is the meaning of love?' and she would look quizzically into his eyes and say, '*Meri jaan*, love has its own unique voice, spoken in universal tones.'

Poetry was the forte of both, and Ghalib and Faiz were their favourites. They would recite to each other and then dissect their core meaning. She lightened up the evenings, singing her own verses, which he loved. Her soft, lilting notes intoxicated him. 'I love your poetry, every word of it. There is philosophy in love here,' he would tell her. The broken pieces of his life were coming together.

Locked in his princess's arms he told her simply that his wife would never let him go. 'She is a cold and calculating woman, but a break-up will destroy her; security is everything for her. She will destroy the child as well. That is how she will seek her revenge. One thing she does very well is hate.' Without breaking away from his grip, she told him, 'I am single, I am a free woman with a child who loves me unconditionally. I am all she has.' Her eyes gleamed and she continued, 'I can still love you with all the intensity in my body, till my bones ache. I can hold you at my own will, and release you when you desire to leave me.'

The man's eyes welled up with emotion and he turned his face away so she would not see his tears. He had never known such love before. But there was fear painted on his face, etched like a permanent tattoo. Now, more than ever before, turning back was not an option.

A CONSUMING CULT

The front door banged and Bangash stormed out angrily. Zubeida collapsed on the kitchen chair and held her dizzy head. A pile of utensils in the kitchen pleaded to be washed. Her mind felt stone dead and she knew that by nightfall she would have a searing headache. Her husband's sudden outburst announcing that he was leaving her for good had defied explanation. He had actually never belonged to her, being always distant, uncaring and aloof.

The bell rang and she dragged herself to the door. In the doorway, blurred by the glaring light of the sun, stood her friend and neighbour, Halima. 'I heard a commotion in your house and dropped by to see what was wrong.' She looked dismayed when she saw Zubeida's crumpled clothes and tear-stained face. 'What has happened? You look like you have been through a wringer.'

'*Haye*, Halima, my world has turned upside down today! That bastard, Bangash, has walked out on me, abandoning the children and me - not that he ever belonged to us, or contributed much to the house. You know, I have supported the family by teaching at a school,' Zubeida flopped helplessly on a chair, 'but the presence of my husband and the father of my children is important, as you well know.'

Zubeida sat hunched at the table, distractedly cracking her bony knuckles in a rhythmic motion, whilst Halima looked on sympathetically. 'I always told you, Zubeida, to control this man. He is a bastard! I swear he will rue this day when he deserted such a lovely wife and family!' Then as an afterthought, she asked, 'By the way, where has he gone?'

There was a pause before Zubeida whispered, 'He has married a woman from the *darbar*.'

'What?' shouted her friend, 'I can't believe this madness, even from a rascal like him!'

'Halima, he was at the *darbar* day and night. He had sworn allegiance to the *Pir*, saying that he is omniscient and that he possesses divine qualities. In a nutshell, his faith in the *Pir* is absolute.' She shook her head muttering, '*Istaghfirullah*! God have mercy on him! It was no worship he did there, it is like a harem. He called the women there *devis* saying that they are the centre of procreation. He is the Devil's disciple!'

Halima looked aghast, 'What kind of worship is this? It's a downright sin!'

Halima was stricken with pity for her dear friend. She glanced around at the house which wore a neglected look. It was shabby and poorly furnished. It lacked the warmth of a home. She could not bear it a minute longer. She rose, embraced her friend and said reassuringly, 'I beg your leave now, Zubeida. I will return again later. Please keep up your spirits for your sake and for the children. Things will sort out with time - they always do. You are in it together - you and the children - they are your biggest support.'

'You are a true friend, Halima. You alone understand my situation,' Zubeida gratefully squeezed her hand. 'Please Halima, keep this to yourself, you know how people talk. Our situation is miserable, and we don't need it to be made worse by others.'

That evening when the children came home, Zubeida broke the news to them. Abrar, her elder son, was outraged. Her daughter, Huma, broke into tears. Disconsolate and broken-hearted herself, she tried to console them, 'He will come to see you sometimes. You never know, he might even return one day.'

Abrar lambasted her angrily, 'This really is the last straw. I am ashamed to call him my father! He is nothing but a deserter.'

'Hush, Abrar, you must not speak of your father like that,' Zubeida admonished, gently taking his hand.

Abrar shook off her hand angrily, 'Amma, you were too compliant, and this is the reason he abused you all these years. Callous people like him take advantage of vulnerability all the time. He has treated us like scum of the earth.' Hysterical with rage, he screamed, 'Answer me! What have you got in return for your loyalty? Zero respect, zero loyalty, zero love!'

Zubeida almost choked on her words, 'I did it for you, my dearest children. If it had happened earlier, it would have destroyed you both. I had to endure it for your sake.'

Huma burst into tears, 'Amma, I don't understand either you or father. I feel utterly, completely betrayed. The two of you are selfish and have never loved us enough to keep us together!'

Her children's words hurt Zubeida to the core. She understood her daughter's anger and that she was torn between love for her father and pain at his rejection. She felt her son's grief as well - he had grown up with suppressed anger. He was revolted by his father's philandering ways and could not forgive him. He had been a precocious child and overnight he seemed to have skipped his childhood and turned serious. He handled domestic affairs like a patriarch in his father's absence. She knew that underneath his manly exterior was deep resentment, grief and anger.

Zubeida's days and nights became a nightmare. She lamented her wasted life. Her commitment to her husband had proved futile and gained her nothing. She wistfully recalled her youthful days when she bubbled over with gaiety and laughter. She had been pretty, with high cheekbones, white glowing skin and sparkling light brown eyes. When she turned eighteen she fell in love with a handsome boy with sharp chiselled features, smiling eyes and slim long fingers. Unfortunately, her parents had disapproved of him. He was an artist, and they considered him to be a wastrel and incapable of supporting their daughter. She was heartbroken but grieved in silence.

Then Bangash had appeared on the scene, full of manly vigour and gusto - a successful trader. Her parents were delighted when he proposed and consented immediately to the marriage of their daughter to him. Zubeida was not attracted to him physically, but limited choices compelled her.

Years later, she regretted marrying this cold and calculating man. He could never love her or any human being except himself. Her life turned into a monotonous drudge. There had been fights when he would leave the house and not return for days. Then when he would finally appear, he would not be penitent and would offer no explanation. She knew that he visited the darbar and suspected something was greatly amiss, but kept her silence.

Weeks passed after Bangash left this time. Zubeida's curiosity peaked and she wanted to visit the darbar. She took Halima into her confidence and they went together. Shrouded in *chaddars*, the women made their way to the *darbar*, an ominous looking place located in an inconspicuous corner and flanked by tall, dilapidated buildings. The exterior was painted in gaudy colours and multi-coloured lights were strung on the surrounding streets. At the gate security personnel asked for proof of identity. They said that they had come to pay homage to the *Pir Sahib* and were relieved that no further questions were asked.

Once inside they found themselves in a courtyard decorated with cheap, colourful paper hangings. The air was heavy with the smoke of *agarbatis*. In a far corner a few women were assembled, chanting and bent in worship. Incantations sounded like the low rumble of thunder. There was magic in the air as devotees moved in a hypnotic and rhythmic trance. A man was beating a drum and dancing, his body whirling to the hypnotic music.

The two moved towards the enclosure for women. Halima asked a young woman telling a rosary, 'Where is the *Pir*? I would like to pay my respects.' The woman answered cautiously in a stifled voice, 'He will be here shortly.'

They waited patiently - time was on hold. A man stepped forward and announced the *Pir's* arrival. An inner door opened and a coterie of men, half-bowing, appeared in the arched doorway. After them a tall man in flowing robes and a turban walked with a sluggish gait towards the dais. He scrutinized the crowd and with a condescending wave of his hand, asked them to be seated. Men and women in turns went up to the *Pir*, kissed his large moist hand, bowed and backed out. Amongst the crowd were disabled children, elderly men and women with sick emaciated bodies to whom he benevolently gave a spoonful of a healing potion. He was known to be a hakim - a healer of those sick in mind and body.

Zubeida and Halima were the last to approach the *Pir*. When it was Zubeida's turn to pay her respects, she bent to kiss his hand and felt his penetrating gaze strip her body. The *Pir* has an eye for women she thought and shuddered. The two women withdrew respectfully, mingling with the congregation and searched for the exit. Bangash was nowhere in sight. The two women left.

Zubeida was in a daze by the time she reached home, haunted by the day's events. She relived the scene at the *darbar* in her mind. She remembered her husband's daily visits there, where he went like a lover to his beloved. When he was home with them his mind and heart were elsewhere. For years she had lived with a man who was only physically present with her. She had felt the pain of his growing indifference.

At the *darbar* today she finally understood the man who had been her husband for many years. His dark brooding mood stood stark in her mind. She had lost him long ago, but had held on to her illusions as her only solace. The pain that gnawed at her was too deep to surface. His desertion was inevitable - delayed, but final like a death knell. Her mind was finally at rest and an inner peace settled on her.

Occasionally Bangash dropped by the house and unapologetically lounged around making small talk with his children. He ignored Zubeida as if she didn't exist for him. She watched him from a distance, motionless and silent. His figure was lean and an unkempt appearance spoke volumes about his condition. Once he offered a paltry amount of money to the children which they instantly refused. 'No! We don't need it,' they said emphatically. He looked stunned and began to speak but stifled his voice and left the house. Zubeida's heart swelled with pride for her children. They had grown up to be self-reliant and had integrity.

The wounds Bangash had inflicted on his family healed with time. Zubeida taught at a local school and earned enough to provide for her children. They could face any crisis as long as they were together. They had learnt that from a very early age. Bangash's black moods and his betrayal built up their resilience. In time, Abrar got a good job and earned a decent salary, and the house that had known nothing but privation became financially stable.

She remembered the last time Bangash had come to see them on one of those routine visits to his children. He stayed longer than he had on previous occasions and looked reluctant to leave. His previous visits were mere protocol and meant to assuage his guilt. This time it was different. He showed keen interest in Abrar and Huma, going over their latest activities. His aging face glowed when Abrar announced his promotion at his office. How easy, thought Zubeida, it was to lap up the triumph of his son's achievements. Huma veered to him easily, as she had always done. It made Zubeida wonder how they had almost gotten over their resentment in their eagerness to please him. She had not planted the seed of hate in them, lest it consume them. When he stood to take his leave, they respectfully saw him out and he turned to look back with an impassive face. Paternal love is strong in its endurance, thought Zubeida. Over their children's heads their eyes met. There was a finality in his look.

A few days later something happened that would change Zubeida's life forever. It was a bright sunny day after a long spell of heavy rains. There was an urgent knock on the door and it seemed that the visitor was in a hurry. Opening the door, she saw a pallid looking woman. She was tall but lean, her flesh shriveled. She gave Zubeida a long penetrating look. Beside her, nervously clutching her hand, was a lean looking boy who stood shy and fearful.

The woman asked diffidently, 'May I enter?' Without answering, Zubeida ushered her in.

'I will not mince my words, madam. I am Elena, Bangash's wife.'

Zubeida's face fell, jolted into shock. Sudden anger welled up, like boiling magma. 'How do you have the audacity to come into my house? After all you are the one who stole my husband from me!'

'I did not exactly steal him from you, he…never really belonged to either of us…' her voice descended into a guttural sound.

The two women stood face to face, one aggressive, the other passive, but partners in some strange way. These two women shared a precious commonality - the bed of the same man. Feelings of jealousy and rage, long contained, erupted in Zubeida's mind -resentment at being rejected and humiliated by the man who was her husband.

The other woman was quiet, her face passive and subdued as if suffering had sucked all emotion out of her. She spoke quietly in a low voice. 'He is dead now. Nothing matters anymore, for the dead are buried and gone. It is all in the past.'

A cry escaped Zubeida's lips. Although she had thought for some time that Bangash might be dead, hearing it from this woman hurt again. 'Is he really dead?' she asked in a low voice.

'Yes, he died in strange circumstances - it doesn't really matter.' Then she continued in a dull voice, 'This is Jehangir, his son, our son.'

Zubeida looked at the quiet boy. She was startled to see he had his father's eyes, as did Abrar.

And now the other woman continued in a dead tone, 'Please, Zubeida, I have come to give this child to your care. I am a poor woman and do not have the means to raise him. You know too well Bangash's ways. He was broke and left me penniless. Please! Oh please! Save his blood from ruination. Remember, it is the same blood that flows in your children's veins.'

Zubeida froze. She pulled herself up, picked up the frightened child and embraced him. His body was cold and unresponsive. On impulse, she held him tight, her mind in a turmoil. She turned around to face the other woman. The spot where she had stood was empty. She was gone with the wind, the way she had come. With a tumult of mixed emotions, she gently led the child inside.

A DAUGHTER'S QUAGMIRE

The daughter had been acting in an odd manner lately, and though the mother could not really place it, she knew that things were changing between them.

The girl was distant and lost in her own world. She was a robust girl, loquacious and vibrant, who infused a spring-like fresh energy into the house. The mother knew all young girls fantasized in their own world that was removed from the real world around them. She was aware that the young learnt in their own time and well-intentioned efforts to teach them about the realities of the world were often met with resistance.

That day the daughter had come home late and rushed straight to her bedroom. The mother followed her but the daughter shut the door in her face. 'Gulbahar, open the door, darling,' the mother called, knocking on the door. The door finally opened a crack, the daughter peeped out and cried sullenly, 'What is it, Mother?' The mother stared at her. 'Gulbahar, don't you know what time it is? It's an unearthly hour to come home. May I ask where you have been?' The daughter stamped her foot, 'Mother, when will you stop coddling me, I am grown up now. It was you who always told me that we were born free and will die free.' The mother was shaken by this reminder but put on a stern face. 'Please Gulbahar, follow the rules of this house while you're living here. Don't treat it like a hotel.' The daughter sighed and was on the verge of saying something but then decided against it. 'Okay, I am sleepy right now, can't it wait till tomorrow?' And the door shut in her face. The mother walked down the corridor looking crushed.

The next day the daughter told her she was in a relationship. She knew the boy from her school days. He came from a lower income background; his father was an electrician and his mother a seamstress. The mother was jolted by her worst fears. 'Darling, firstly you are too young to marry. You haven't completed college yet. Have you thought how incomplete your life will be without that education? And what will you do later on in life? Marriage is not the be all and end all of life, it is one of the many passageways we walk through. And then marrying a boy from a lower income family, whose future is dubious, makes me uncomfortable.' Her daughter was outraged and burst into tears. 'Mother you consider me incapable of making my own decisions! And you are such a snob and very pretentious if you think they are not good enough for me. What makes us better than them? I am disappointed in you!'

The mother was at her wits' end. 'Darling you are too young to understand, marriage is not all about romance. It's a difficult task all the way. It is ironic that the biggest decisions of our life are made on impulse. Look at me! I made the decision to marry, again on sheer impulse, defying the wishes of my family, and look where I ended up, getting a divorce.' The daughter was silent and knew her mother had been left out in the cold by her parents, and later abused by her cold and calculating husband, but she was convinced that it would be different for her. 'Mother, one wrong doesn't make another wrong, otherwise life wouldn't move on, you should know better. My would-be husband is passionately and deeply in love with me. He says our love is all that matters, we don't need anybody else. And I believe every word he says, implicitly and absolutely!' The daughter, whose brown curly ringlets tossed defiantly in the air, was distraught, and it wrung her mother's heart.

The mother knew her daughter could not be deterred. She pleaded with her to give it some more time and thought, but for the young girl time was running out. Adolescent love is wild and ferocious and licked by wildfires, and there was no abating it. The mother was torn between love for her daughter and the need to caution her, but she finally relented with a sinking heart. She knew she was becoming irrelevant in her precious daughter's life.

After a brief ceremony, hastily arranged, and a gathering of few guests, the daughter was married. The mother saw them off as they impatiently departed for their honeymoon. When she kissed her daughter farewell, she said, 'I wish you a happy marriage. Take care of yourself.' The daughter responded ecstatically, 'I will mother! Thank you for everything.' The mother turned her face away so her daughter could not see her tears. The young couple looked jubilant. They had achieved their goal, their lives were complete. During their honeymoon they lived in a capsule, far away from the eyes of the world. Each day was spent in a trance-like joy.

When the honeymoon was over, things returned to normal. The sheer bliss was unsustainable and slowly diminished. Reality began with daily mundane chores that were at first a novelty but soon grew arduous, and later pure grinding drudgery. Small, trivial skirmishes exploded, irked like an uneasy conscience. The baggage that they carried from their previous lives swelled and reared its ugly head. The boy had a patriarchal mind-set, the girl was a libertarian. He wanted control, power and authority, and she felt small and degraded and yearned for a carefree life. Youth and inexperience proved to be a lethal cocktail, adding to the turmoil. At first, when squabbles flared up they were quickly reconciled. Then they started to linger and fester and sores began to show. The girl's pretty face showed signs of weariness and fatigue. The husband was wracked by anxiety. They laughed less and there were long periods of unbroken silence before any flimsy resolution emerged. Fault lines erupted in their relationship and dreams came hurtling down.

The mother sensed her daughter's distress and was grieved. She lingered in the shadows and waited for the drama to unfold. Her daughter had broken free from her and no longer belonged to her. There were walls, tangible and intangible, between them that could not be dismantled. The mother had to respect her daughter's newly created space. She knew there were limits to anybody's endurance, especially her daughter's. And then there was destiny that was being written by her daughter in her own handwriting. The mother sensed her own dilemma; standing on the outside she could see everything inside. And yet she held herself back and waited for the wind to turn.

The couple fought, wrangled, and became estranged from each other. The mother and daughter, who had become distant, moved closer again. All the while, the husband feared that his future with his wife might take a disastrous turn and that he might lose her altogether. Times had undergone a metamorphosis since his father's times. Values had changed and the ethics that held his parent's marriage did not hold today. The ground under his feet was slipping, and his future was uncertain and rudderless. Cupid's wings lay limp and in tatters at his feet and his will to mend things slackened.

A FATAL EMBRACE

'She has a pretty face, but this Anjuman is twice the size of my poor Ghauri,' Majida muttered under her breath, screwing her narrow eyes to take a closer look at the photograph of a young girl. Like most of the girls in the bundle of photographs lying in Majida's lap, she was decked up beyond her years and was smiling broadly in an innocent yet flirtatious manner hoping to please a prospective mother-in-law and groom. But alas, she had committed the fatal mistake of selecting a photographer who did not have the skills to portray her in a flattering light!

As Majida made a mental note to warn her friends to dispatch better photographs next time, Humayun, her tall, burly husband with a distinctive Hercule Poirot moustache, stepped into the room.

'There you are, looking as carefree as ever,' Majida said with forced sarcasm.

'Now! Now! It's too early in the day for you to start picking a fight,' he replied with a grin, his moustache becoming more prominent.

'You are never serious about things. Ghauri is heading to America in less than six months and you're not at all concerned about getting him married before then. Or at least engaged!'

Humayun burst into laughter—it was a loud guffaw that was characteristic of him.

'*Tauba*! When you laugh like this, it makes me go mad!' Majida exclaimed.

'He has barely finished his medical degree. Let him go to the US and complete his residency in peace there,' he said, knowing very well that his words fell on deaf years. Then he added with a twinkle in his eye, 'And let your son have a bit of fun in America before you bury him in the holy shrine of marriage.'

'He can develop a roving eye and pick a *gori* for a wife. He is young and handsome, any girl can fall for him,' Majida continued.

'You are incorrigible, my dearest wife. Is this all your son will think of as soon as he lands on the shores of America? Give him some credit for a little maturity.'

'I don't comprehend men. You ought to know better,' his wife said with exasperation.

'You don't need to comprehend men. But you can at least try to know your own son,' Humayun said, as he sat on the chair next to his wife. 'Times have changed, my dear. We shouldn't force what we want on our kids, especially not on Ghauri. He's reserved, docile and too young. He can never say no to you. And you know that too well.'

'He listens to me because he trusts me,' she retorted.

'He listens to you and that's good. But that doesn't mean he's your pet puppy.'

'*Acha*, don't pontificate all the time,' Majida said, as she got up from her chair stiffly - she had been sitting there for the last hour. The arthritis was getting to her on a daily basis, but it couldn't ever destroy her spirit. She had the toughness of a man yet the heart of a woman, or so she liked to believe.

As she sauntered out of the room, Humayun's eyes followed her. After all these years, he still loved her - her constant prattle, her warm beauty, her vigour for life. Yet no one tested his patience more than she did with her irritating quality of poking her nose into everybody's affairs. She was in the habit of dropping into neighbours' houses for a casual cup of tea without warning. People tolerated her for her warmth and affection which spilled over into everything she did. At home she was the central figure and was upset if treated otherwise. With time the family learnt to comply with her demands to maintain domestic harmony.

A special quality that endeared her to the family was her unequivocal support and they could depend on her for being there for them and protecting them. She was adept at manipulating people around her, and just when they began to feel too secure in her love, she would tear them to pieces. Nobody dared to disobey her as she was ruthlessly unforgiving and adroit in emotional blackmail. Majida brazenly told the world that she had a wonderful obedient family, when all the latter desired was to be left in peace, and this they accomplished by putting up a show of deferential compliance.

'Oh well,' Humayun murmured to himself, as he twirled his moustache.

Majida was true to her word. Within a fortnight she managed to find a girl for her son. The girl's name was Mira. Tall, pretty, fair-skinned and well-groomed, she fitted into the criteria of a perfect bride. Her father was a bureaucrat, well known to many, and the mother came from a family of old wealth and moved in the right circles. All the conditions were checked off.

There was one obstacle left in Majida's mind—Ghauri's consent. When Ghauri was asked, he deferred the decision to his parents, and the father, after a bit of huff and puff, deferred the decision to his wife. Consequently, overcoming this obstacle turned out to be simpler than expected. The formalities were dealt with between the two families and the couple was swiftly engaged, but of course with much ado.

A few weeks after the engagement, as Majida lounged in her living room, Ghauri, tall, dark and lanky, entered the room with a beaming smile.

'*Merejaan*! You look so happy,' Majida said, matching her son's smile.

'Well, I must confess you have made a good choice, Amma,' he said with a grin.

'Now you know you can always rely on your mother's choice,' Majida said proudly. 'Anyway, where is she these days? I haven't seen her for a while.'

'She's gone to Karachi for a shoot.'

'Shoot?' Majida looked puzzled.

'Just a song shoot! Her friend's written this song and he wanted her to be in the video,' Ghauri replied. He quickly realised he had said more than he should have.

'That's not nice. Good girls don't put themselves on display like this,' Majida said, shifting her voluminous body in her chair, the discomfort showing in her voice.

'Oh, don't worry about it. No need to be this conservative.'

'Frankly, I don't even like that she works in media. Who knows how the men at her workplace behave! Are you not aware of workplace harassment these days?' Majida continued, her mind wandering off into dangerous terrains.

'Uff, you and your old-fashioned beliefs! You can't expect her to sit idle at home and be like all those gossiping housewives,' he said, visibly annoyed.

'Don't talk to me like that!' Majida checked her son. 'What's wrong with being a housewife? I'm a housewife, and you should be grateful for that, otherwise I don't know what messed up juvenile you would have turned out to be.' Then she added sharply, 'I'm your mother.

There is no need to be defensive about your fiancée with me.' Ghauri shook his head, brooding darkly, but chose to be silent.

As the wedding date drew nearer, there was tension in the air as Majida made it clear that she was not happy with the match. Repeated allusions to the girl's 'interesting' career were made in social gatherings and wedding planning between the two families would unfold into convoluted debates, and mere small talk would inevitably erupt into heated arguments.

Then one morning, when the marriage was barely a month away, Majida announced to Humayun, 'Last night I dreamt that the celebratory red of the wedding suddenly turned into blood, and the orange colour of the mehndi transformed into a huge fire that consumed our house. This is a very bad omen. We must cancel the wedding!' Majida said with fear and urgency.

'You can't do that!' protested Humayun.

'Would you rather that we suffer later on, instead of breaking it off at this stage?' Majida exclaimed, her eyes brimming with tears.

'Ask Ghauri first, before you take any such action,' he said in a desperate tone, struck by foreboding.

'No, he won't understand. I need to do it for his sake. Please, don't stop me,' said Majida, as she burst into tears.

Humayun fell silent. He could never win an argument with her, so he kept his silence. The same day the engagement was called off, very abruptly but with composure, as if it was the most normal thing in the world.

Ghauri was in a fit of rage and indignation. He stamped into his mother's room. 'Amma, why did you have to break off the engagement? How could you!'

Majida was taken aback as Ghauri had never shouted at her. 'I did it for your sake, son. You don't know how terrible the dream was. Our lives were about to be consumed in fire. I will never let any harm come to you or my family, not over my dead body! You know…'

'For heaven's sake, Amma!' interrupted Ghauri. 'Stop this drama. Who gives a damn about your superstitions! I love Mira!'

'You don't love her. It was just infatuation or lust,' she continued blithely. 'I'll find another tall, fair-skinned and beautiful girl for you. Why there is no dearth of pretty girls. Any girl will be happy to marry you. You are such a catch my son, a very eligible bachelor indeed.'

'Eligible bachelor, indeed!' Then with a trembling voice, he added, 'I can never face Mira. She thinks we are a crazy bunch of lunatics and the sad thing is she's absolutely right!' He wanted to break down and sob but held back. For the first time, he was thoroughly incensed at his mother's behaviour and was at the end of his tether.

As Ghauri left the room, Majida breathed a heavy sigh. 'This anger will pass,' she muttered under her breath, as she adjusted her dupatta. Majida would never realise how she had wounded her son. Much as he loved her, he could not forgive her for ruining his life, even if it was inadvertently.

Ghauri would never forget the desolate look on Mira's face when she confronted him about their broken engagement. She had burst out angrily, 'Ghauri, you have hurt me more than you can imagine. And more than the hurt, it is the humiliation I will carry with me always. People will blame me, my name will be smeared whilst you walk away unblemished. Shame on you!'

A few weeks later, on a cold winter morning, Ghauri left for the US. He was quiet and sullen and the goodbyes with his parents were chilly and distant. Humayun and Majida looked contrite, but the ice could not be broken. For months afterwards, Humayun and Majida barely heard from their son. Ghauri called Humayun a couple of times, talked briefly, informing him of his well-being, but before Majida could take the phone, he would drop the line. Time passed and Majida became more reclusive and talked sparingly, her distinctive chatter giving way to a tense and solemn expression that hung in the air like a dense fog. A portion of herself had been severed from her and she looked bereft.

Then one day Humayun received a brief letter from his son. It read abruptly, 'Abba, last week I married Sophie, an American emigrant. We are very happy. I would have broken the news to Amma, but you know her, she will tear me to pieces. Please inform her about this. I am sorry but it was all done in a rush, so there was no time to call and tell you.'

Humayun nervously handed Majida the letter. She held it for five minutes, and read it again and again, with a blank expression. 'I don't know what to say,' Humayun said, as he stared at Majida, trying to break the silence. A part of him was happy for his son, but at the same time he felt sympathy for his wretched wife, who was still clutching to a forlorn hope of getting her son back. He expected her to convulse into a spasm of rage or hysteria. He was taken aback when Majida's blank expression gave way to a wry smile. Then she suddenly said with a flicker of her old fire, 'Are you going to keep standing there with that idiotic expression on your face, or get moving? We need to get the next flight to America. Your sly son has gotten married without telling us. Now I need to check out what lunatic he's picked out for himself.' Humayun's tense expression gave way to a guffaw as he said, 'Majida! Majida! You are incorrigible!'

A MAN OF GOD

The tall gaunt man with a red headscarf and a flowing white robe stood at the podium brandishing his hands wildly. His blue eyes glinted with passion as his rhetoric became louder. A striking picture in the whole scenario was the spectators, sitting patiently on the sprawling field. They listened in silence, awestruck by the oratory of this inscrutable man. Whether they fully understood him or not, they sat and listened in rapt attention.

The man, whose name was Haider Ali, had lived in isolation for many years in a foreign country and now appeared out of nowhere like a jack-in-the-box. He stood before them in flesh and blood, like a true warrior of the soil heading an army. His rhetoric was a distant call for those whose hearts beat with frenzied faith. It was a stunning feat of wits on the part of this man who magnetically pulled a huge crowd at a single call. People from all over the land, from small hamlets to big cities, had travelled to Islamabad. The crowd belonged to the low economic strata of society whose stakes were higher. The dismal situation of their lives drove them to nurse a forlorn hope for a better life.

Overhead, dense clouds gathered, threatening rain. The crowd appeared undaunted, with no intention to take shelter. The man at the podium continued to bellow, inspired by the rolling sea of people. He shouted like a delirious man, 'My dear brethren, bless you all. My heart goes out to you, the browbeaten people and victims of men who make slaves out of you. I am here as your saviour, to rescue you from the vicious fangs of the serpent whose poison has devoured you for too long. God has sent me to help you, I, who have the ability to perform this great task. You and I shall rise together, and if be it, fall together.'

The crowd listened, huddled in the cold, mesmerized by his voice. The temperature dipped to freezing, and above there was thunder and the skies growled. Nature was in no mood to be pacified. The teeming crowd was an odd medley of raggedly dressed men, women and children of all ages. A week ago, word had spread that the cleric had ordered them to join a procession using children as human shields against the powerful men who had led them to ruin and damnation.

The man bellowed with ferocious energy, shady motives uncoiling in his fevered brain. His audience sat like dumb robots with gaping mouths. He raised his thunderous voice to jolt their sluggish hearts and minds.

'Awake my countrymen! Rise to the hour! Until you rise, no wind shall blow, no leaf shall stir, no seed shall grow from this soil. Strike a flame in your hearts and let it burn. You shall then witness God's miracle when He comes down to help you. Rise and fight the oppressor. Light the fire of revolt so that perpetrators may be consumed!'

This was followed by a deafening applause and cries from ignorant people who were ready to believe anything. They had lived in hardship for too long and now hope limped forlornly.

The man at the podium continued, 'You must fight for liberty even in the face of death. In the not too distant past, your parents gave their blood for the birth of a new state. Now, once again, your blood will make this land fertile and will feed your future generations. I shall stand in your midst, nay stand in front of you, so their bullets riddle my body before they do yours!' The crowd trembled with emotion.

Finally, exhausted after his intense oratory, he climbed into his container, a temporary built-in room on wheels, made to accommodate him on this great day. As he settled into his enormous armchair, he could feel his old bones creak with fatigue. His wife served him a cup of steaming hot tea, 'Dear, didn't you overdo it this time?' she queried. He replied vaguely, 'I have a debt to pay. Now, my dear wife, bring me something to eat.'

She served him a hot spicy meal of chicken that he devoured. He could not conceal a wry smile. His eyes gleamed as he surveyed the container he had set up for this great day. It was furnished with plush sofas and accessories including a stove, microwave oven and a small refrigerator. He admired the perfect heating system fitted into it. It had cost him a fortune, but then he knew his old limbs could not do without these essentials. After all, he deserved nothing less - the supreme saviour of the people. Everyone has his moment in the sun, he thought, with his days of anonymity behind him. The crowd sat outside in the cold, whimpering like orphaned children. Word had gone round and taken root that he was a man of God, sent to deliver them and feed them luscious fruits from paradise.

And then providence intervened. The dark and somber skies finally shed their heavy burden. Rain poured, filling the crevices. The mob, cold and soaking wet, now began to disperse. With one roar they marched and soon turned on each other. Their hearts were by now boiling with anger, fired by their wretched condition. What they had held inside finally poured out like poison. Having listened attentively to the voice of revolt, their hearts were ignited.

They drew their pistols and whatever other weapons they had from under their garments and fell upon each other with savage vengeance. Bullets whizzed in all directions like fireworks. Pools of blood collected in potholes in clotted heaps.

A wave of insanity overwhelmed them like an epileptic seizure. Their tongues hung out like mad dogs. Boys, barely beyond puberty, aimed their slingshots randomly in the air. Others picked up stones and hurled them at standing cars. They became complicit in this game of make belief; this mad war game that would leave only dead men behind, and for the survivors a dream-like illusion of victory.

The roads were littered with dead men, wounded men, and screaming women and infants. A man stood up, hoisted a flag splattered with wet dirt. Jumping up and down he cried, 'All praise to the cleric! He is the hero of the hour!'

The crowd roared approval, echoing his slogans, 'All praise to God!' There was madness in the air, turning uglier by the hour. The man at the podium had excavated an ogre of beast-like rage, buried deep within them, laid them bare and naked. Once out in the open, it was impossible to contain this flash flood.

Their madness peaked and then abruptly faded as sanity returned. They looked to the podium, seeking a new direction. It was empty. The man was gone, vanished like a spectre in the darkness. If they had only looked earlier to the dais, they would have seen the man in the red scarf scurrying away like a frightened mouse. Having accomplished his mission, he did not hesitate to make his speedy exit. He shrank from witnessing the carnage he had provoked. Where they should go from here, neither he nor they had any idea.

The crowd drifted like the wind having lost its speed. Their energy was sapped like sick men with their vitality sucked out. Nobody could have imagined that these men who were part of that violent, murderous gang could be transformed magically into ordinary everyday people. They had shed their masks and became ordinary citizens who spend their regular days in labour. The spirit of the devil had inhabited them temporarily, upset their balance and then, with a wicked grimace, had left, perhaps to return another day with fresh vengeance.

The man in the red scarf had trudged along in the dark to his house, situated a furlong away from this arena. He appeared satisfied with himself as he stroked his thick moustache, giving himself a pat on the back for the feat he had accomplished that day. Those fools had swallowed everything, he thought. It had been easy. All he had done was a bit of research and polished his rhetoric. His skills at oratory had been honed from the time he preached at a local school. There his young pupils had revered him. All he did now was build a sacred image of himself, climb a pulpit, and then let his tongue wag like a frisky dog.

He shut the doors and windows of his house, spread a mat on the ground and prayed before he fell into a restless slumber. His night was disturbed by nightmares, but his soul slept on.

He was woken in the early hours of the morning by the sound of a loud uproar. He jumped out of bed and hastened to the window. Nervously pulling up one shutter he saw a sea of people, restively assailing the front of his house. They were brandishing sticks in the air and lamenting loudly.

His first impulse was to escape from the back door into a back alley where no one could find him. Then sanity took the better of him and with outward composure he cautiously opened the front door. Before him stood a mob with faces twisted in anger. His heart cringed, 'Is the day of retribution knocking at my door?'

They heard him say, 'My brethren! I was forced to take my leave yesterday against my will. I assure you, my heart broke to see you standing unsheltered in the cold, wet night. I wanted you to go home and rest.' He looked around for assurance, but before he could speak, the mob heaved like a huge elephant struck by its foe. Their cup of patience was empty. Two men lunged at him, clawed at his face and body. One of them shouted, 'Come on, my fellas! Let's raid his house.' And with one big push they rushed into his house, smashed the furniture and tore at the drapes, smashing the windows. On the walls hung photographs of the cleric looking down with a mocking smile, that they tore into pieces.

These men knew they had been cheated the previous night. Their self-proclaimed saint had abandoned them in their hour of trial. The blood of their dear brethren was on his hands. How could they forgive him after he had let their blood choke the city's drains?

Their revenge taken, the mob poured out of the house and dispersed into the many lanes in the city. Sounds of laughter and loud talk were heard as they buried themselves in the humdrum of their city life. They went home and cuddled their children and made love to their wives as if nothing had happened. Memory is short-lived in those destitute of mind and body.

When the wretched man saw the last of them go, he summoned the energy to rise. His limbs were bleeding and ached with excruciating pain that lacerated his body. His clothes were torn and exposed his naked body. He thanked God he was alive. The brutes could have killed him. This was what the saviour had gotten in return for his largesse. They wanted him to die fighting for them. Leaders never gave up their lives - who then would hold a torch for these ignorant, good-for-nothing folks?

With heavy steps, he slunk into the house and collapsed on the ground. His wife screamed, horrified to see his bloody appearance. His clothes were torn and blood was oozing from wounds. She tended to his lacerations and lay him down. A comely yet shrewd woman, she took it all in. She prepared chicken broth for him and fed him herself.

He barely heard her as she scolded him, 'You have made a fool of yourself today. For God's sake, never repeat this buffoonery again. Take my word for it. You think you are a saviour of the people. Be damned! You have condemned yourself to a life of ignominy. If you didn't have the gumption to face them, then why whip up their passion? They could have killed you tonight.'

The old man, too tired to argue, kept his peace but growled under his breath, 'Ignorant woman be damned!' and having said this, turned his back and fell into a deep slumber.

A PECULIAR MAN

He was a frequent visitor at a popular club in the city, this man of multiple shades, conspicuous by his aloof, standoffish manner. On some days he was seen in the company of friends and colleagues, but on others he would be found seated in a corner by himself. Whether he interacted with people or not depended on his impulse-driven mood. Friends and strangers alike left him to his own devices. Occasionally he would engage in discourse with great robustness, gesticulating and going to and forth, eager to get his message across. He liked to win every argument. This naturally did not go down well with people in general and he ruffled feathers, but he couldn't care less!

For all his weird attributes, it was apparent that he was an elusive man who shunned company. His life was not run-of-the-mill, as many people's lives are. He had contempt for such people, the spineless sheep, bleating to the tune of others. For him there were no role models and none worthy to emulate. He himself was a jewel in the crown, the quintessential being standing alone who, whether happy or tortured, lived for himself. He was a lover of literature and music, frequenting the various musical and literary events the city had to offer. He dabbled in the arts and wrote articles that were published in local newspapers.

A. K. Hadi was his name. He was a practicing lawyer who drew a mixed reaction from his peers - awe, respect, fear. Tall and lean, he prided himself on being anglicised in speech, dress and deportment. However, his polish easily wore off when he revealed an abrasive tongue. It was a common truism circulated by his colleagues, 'Keep away from Mr Hadi and don't take any liberty with him or he will soon go off the handle!'

Hadi was a criminal lawyer, proficient at handling complex cases in a professional manner. These included blasphemy cases in which religious and minority groups were targeted, and cases about the abuse of women and terrorism. His colleagues admired his grit, yet with a touch of envy. One cynical peer commented, 'This man will live to regret his temerity.' Hadi ignored them; he considered it his duty to enact justice and make society free and equitable. He did not hesitate to prosecute diehard terrorists, who were then punished.

For all his mixed traits, Hadi nurtured grudges. On one occasion he had a falling out with his brother, Faris, a known writer and journalist. Faris had just published an article in a literary journal. Incidentally, Hadi had also sent an article to the same publisher and this was turned down. Hadi was sorely disappointed. He had put a lot of research into his article, but the publisher had declined to print it, declaring it to be too controversial and against the ethics of their journal. Hadi had marched to his brother's house and confronted him saying, 'You have conspired against me and had your paper published. There is nothing original in your article, neither is it as well researched as mine, and yet you have pulled strings and had it printed!'

Faris was appalled. 'What are you talking about? Have you gone crazy! I did no such thing.' But Hadi was in a manic rage and refused to listen, walking out of the room in a fit of anger. Faris watched his brother's receding figure with impotent rage. He muttered to himself, 'Hadi has lost his balance! I fear for him!'

The brothers fell out with each other. Hadi continued to sulk, convinced he was right. Faris carried a chip on his shoulder for the rest of his life, and didn't forgive him. Hadi was in truth an angry man. Where it came from, none knew. His wife, Marie, now separated from him, had for years been in mortal dread of him. For years his paroxysms of rage and whimsical moods stayed in her mind. Every day, when he returned home from work, he would dive behind the newspaper and would remain like that for the entire evening, 'I need some time for myself.' The evenings passed with the two shut in their separate shells.

When it came to intimacy, he was sexually uninhibited. After it was over he would disengage and would walk out of the bedroom to down a glass of brandy. This was the closest they ever came to each other.

While their marriage lasted, Marie had her moments of frustration at being dispensable in his life, an object of no value. His chivalry to other women was a constant irritant. 'Do you ever have time for me? You are striving to impress other women all the time, even strangers.' She exploded, 'Am I less than them, tell me?' Hadi shrugged his shoulders, 'You are too sensitive and up in arms for nothing. Do I have a mistress? Am I seen flirting around in the city? I demand that you get off my back! I can't take such flak from you anymore.'

Years later her single regret was that she did not see the writing on the wall earlier and let herself be tortured for years. The damage would have been less, or not at all. She now suffered constant anxiety.

The only person he truly loved was his daughter, Sana. He loved to stroke her silky hair, kiss her cheeks that glowed like pink blossoms and to spoil her with toys and candies. She was too young for fear in those days. He was possessive and he did not want to lose the only being who belonged to him.

The divorce dragged on, blowing fumes of rage, and there was a fierce tussle over the custody of Sana that Marie pursued doggedly. She won, forcing Hadi to concede. Marie packed her belongings and left for America. Hadi could visit Sana once a year in the States.

The prime of his life was over. Marie had long been gone and taken Sana with her. Alcohol was now his closest ally, it helped to soothe his spirits. His other love, classical music, lulled his mind and elevated his spirits to celestial heights.

One fine morning, Hadi sat in the library of the club, pouring over a piece of paper, engrossed in the serious business of writing a poem. He had been asked to read his poetry at a literary event that evening. His mind worked feverishly as he focused on writing the poem. When he was satisfied, after repeatedly editing it, he folded it neatly and put it in his pocket and walked out of the library.

That evening, as he stood at the podium in the hall, he looked smugly at a sea of faces, an unusual sight at these literary programs that generally drew small crowds. They were here to listen to him read his work. The crowd was a mix of sober old men and eager youth, come to savour an intellectual treat that they still relished, though a rare entity now.

He read in a clear, loud voice as the audience listened attentively. Afterwards there was thunderous clapping. Over a cup of tea and chicken sandwiches, his friends congratulated him. Zafar, an old friend, patted his shoulder and said, 'Well done, Hadi! You have given us a much-needed dose tonight. It was a poem, propitious to the times, a slap in the face of our pompous elite. I enjoyed your cynical allusions tucked into the verses.'

Another friend, Fahim, quietly approached him, saying, 'You are a smart guy, Hadi, you sheathe your arrows whilst you hit the bull's eye. Congratulations! Let us meet up for a drink sometime soon!' Hadi laughed it off, but the applause lifted his spirits.

He was a happy man that day for various reasons - his poetry was heard by many and his lifestyle matched that of any well-to-do person in his town. He was a regular visitor to the popular club and was known to all its exclusive members. He was well-respected within the legal fraternity and his devotion to justice was lauded. He had a lovely daughter who could be the joy of any father - accomplished and with a successful career. Nobody could point a finger at him and say he had failed in life. He had adhered to his principles in the face of many storms. And this was no mean feat.

That evening he went home to his empty house, exhausted after a hectic day. He prepared for the night, donning his silk pyjamas and a loose-fitting shirt, and settled into bed. It was a cold night and there was no heating in the house. As usual now, at night there was no gas to warm the house. He cursed the government for their poor governance.

That night the wind howled and rain fell in a torrential downpour. The house was deathly quiet. He heard a rustling sound outside his window. 'It must be the wind', he said to himself. Then he heard it again. He ignored it, being too tired to get up and investigate. Maybe he imagined it, he thought to himself. With that he drifted into a deep sleep.

There was no one who could have heard Hadi's screams that night and come to his rescue. The intruders broke open a window latch and entered the sleeping man's chamber. At that moment Hadi awoke and shouted, 'Who's there?' Then seeing three men, he screamed loudly. It was then that one of them took out his knife and slashed through the man's neck. He groaned and fell back. A river of blood gushed out of him. One man kicked him viciously in the chest to confirm that he was dead. The other man laughed, 'I have never had it this easy. Just one go at him and he's dead. He was a dead man already!' Then they rolled up their victim in the rug that was by his bed. Having finished their business, they slipped back quietly into the black night.

Two days later a neighbour, noticing there was no activity in the house next door and seeing only a heap of newspapers and mail on the front door, sensed mischief and broke open the door. He was horrified to see the poor man's corpse bundled in a rug. There was blood all over the room. Otherwise nothing in the house had been touched, nothing ransacked or broken. The neighbours called the police, but the murderers had left behind no trail. The case was closed.

After several days had passed an old neighbour had only one comment, 'It happens all the time here, another casualty in a decadent state.'

A STAR THAT BLAZED

The star of the evening was Sangeeta. The auditorium was packed with an animated audience and applause echoed through the hall like the perpetual ringing of temple bells. The dancer, the epitome of grace and agility, held the audience spellbound.

The movements of her body were like the taut strings of a guitar, and she was the focal point on the large stage. Her body sustained a rhythm, *taka takadhintaka dhin*, symmetry and a balance of movement--*dhindhindhadhindhindha*. She was a maestro in the art of Kathak dance that few excelled in now. The music resonated to a high pitch and then descended into low pitch, enveloping her in a trance. The melody, movements and nuanced gestures portrayed the sad story of an ill-fated love. The subcontinent is replete with tragic love stories of Waris Shah, a very popular story being *Heer Ranjha* where star-crossed lovers are doomed to die, unable to consummate their love as they are challenged by a strictly bigoted society where love between a man and woman is condemned, except in the marital realm.

When the music stopped the dancer fell to the floor, signifying the end. The audience gave her a standing ovation as she bowed her way out. She had the capacity to strike at the core of a native, raw, primeval calling. Dance was censored and viewed as being against pristine norms, but this made the charm of watching it a greater pleasure. A guilty pleasure!

When the performance ended, her fans gathered around Sangeeta.

'What expression! *Wah*!'

'Such a fine storyteller you are! One movement of yours speaks a thousand words!'

'You are the pride of our nation. We should throw out these mullahs and have you as our cultural minister.' Hilarious laughter followed this tongue-in-cheek humour. The public hungered for these art forms to calm their thirsty spirit.

Sangeeta's face shone, acclamation from admirers was always gratifying and humbling. 'Thank you, thank you so much,' she said, bowing again.

The night was deepening and the crowd dispersed. Sangeeta rose wearily and slowly walked down the aisle. The excitement of the evening had already blurred and the stimulation had ebbed. Exhausted to her bones, going down the concert hall steps, she heard the sound of running footsteps behind her. It was Taimur! He had been running to catch up and was breathless.

'Hey! Slow down, lady! Get off the high horse you are riding and bring yourself down to the ground. It's over now. They have all gone home and forgotten about you.'

'Wow! You know you are the only man who is forever trying to put me down. With friends like you who needs enemies?' Sangeeta retorted with an exasperated, but pleasant smile.

'Sangeeta ji, at least I'm not like those sycophants. Don't you tire of these hangers-on? You know I'm the only man who sees you as you are. You should appreciate me for holding up a mirror to you.'

'Well, I don't like mirrors.'

Taimur burst out laughing. '*Uff*! You know this is what I like about you: your blunt candour!'

'Oh, come on! I am in no mood for jokes. For once, be serious.'

She turned to Taimur and their gaze locked momentarily. A spark of fizz surfaced. Sangeeta shifted her eyes quickly. Around them was silence, broken by the distant sound of technical staff packing away for the night.

Taimur lit a cigarette, covering it with his hands, and took a long deep puff before he spoke, 'You know you always doubt my sincerity. You would rather I show you a beautiful, flawless image to feed your fattened ego. Oh, and why is the peak so lonely and disquieting?' His voice had a hint of mockery and sadness.

She touched his hand gently and smiled, 'Well it is only with you that I can be myself. You are not shocked at what I say and do. I appreciate your non-judgmental attitude, a mark of true friendship!'

'I don't need to be judgmental. I leave this precious pastime for others. And there are plenty of people who have nothing better to do but to fill their empty pockets with garbage.' They had by now reached Sangeeta's car. 'Do you want to go for a drive? I'll drop you on the way back,' Taimur said with the eagerness of a child not yet ready to leave the playground.

'No, I'm way too tired.'

Disappointed, he replied, 'So, when do I see you again, Sangeeta?'

'Hopefully soon, I have a crazy schedule these days.'

Taimur stared blankly, watching her drive away. Plunged in thought, he stood rooted to the ground for a long time.

'Sangeeta, my little mystery,' he murmured under his breath. Yes, he might share intimate moments with her, but he didn't really know her. Sometimes he felt he knew her better than anyone, and at other times she eluded him. After all, she was a woman who belonged to everybody. She embraced people with the ease of water. They could relate to her, but somewhere, at some point, she distanced herself. She could be their ally, but she met them only half-way. Her friends and associates were disappointed when they embraced an empty space. He wondered if she even knew herself or whether she was in touch with her feelings, for fame has a way of twisting reality. She was a magical woman who embraced fame with humility and love. People who knew her occupied all the spaces within her, leaving her with little space for herself - only emptiness. She was not easy to define in the way people know each other.

His mind strayed into those mysterious labyrinths of her mind where she played games with herself and people, knowingly or unknowingly. 'I wonder if she has been playing games with me all these years,' he murmured to himself. Then he pushed the thought away - perhaps only time would unravel all. He shrugged and forced this dynamic woman out of his mind as she had the power to drive him crazy. Deep down he was a reckless, passionate man, and like this woman he loved, he wanted all or nothing. He wasn't content with drinking from a half-empty cup.

Five miles and a hundred thoughts away, Sangeeta let herself into her palatial home, ghostlike in its hollowness. She walked towards her bedroom, the clinking of her anklets and tapping of her heels were the only sounds piercing the silence. It was the same when she returned home every night. Her private life had shrunk to these few rooms, but this was what she desired. Her solitude was her ally that she embraced devoutly. She became alive only when she performed, for then her true spirit rose out of its depth.

The telephone rang loudly, breaking the silence.

'Hello Sangeeta ji. This is Mohan speaking. You have a concert the day after tomorrow. You will be performing, won't you?'

'Yes, Mohan Sahib, of course,' Sangeeta answered slowly, aware of sleep descending on tired eyelids. She had barely hung up when the telephone rang again.

'Sangeeta, this is Hina. There is a fund-raising ceremony organised by the famous business tycoon, Ahmad Ali. He has asked you to dance at his event. He won't take no for an answer.'

'Well, I will look up my schedule for the following week. I will let you know later.'

'Oh, thank you Sangeeta! Please don't let us down.'

'I will definitely try.'

She placed the telephone down. 'Damn people who are obsequious and coercive at the same time,' she thought aloud, hand on phone, knowing it would ring again. And it did.

'Sangeeta, an international concert of musical performances is being held in London next month. You are the privileged one to be selected from our country. You will have to leave in two weeks.'

'That's wonderful news, but I have commitments. I guess I will have to cancel them. I'll confirm with you later.'

She placed the phone off the hook and moved to her bedroom. Sinking into the chair in front of the dressing table, she removed her jewelry, and looked at her reflection in the mirror. A beautiful doll, decked up from head to toe in a silk sari, *kundan* jewelry, bright red lipstick, and scented *motia* flowers braided in her dark wavy hair. The finishing touch was the thick kajal magnifying her large almond shaped eyes, cleverly distracting from the tell-tale signs of wrinkles circling them.

Life was a whirlwind and she was constantly in motion, like a fish in the open sea. Her admirers who put her on a pedestal made it all worthwhile. There was one constant - loneliness. Like all beautiful artifacts, she was worshipped, but could not be touched. Men flirted with her as if she were an exquisite plaything. The women were worse. They felt threatened by her and with time, distanced themselves. They oscillated between servility and aloofness. They could not relate to successful women. Her mother had told her, 'There is one place at the peak for everyone. It is beautiful, but a very solitary place.' Her mother, who had tasted stardom, had been right, and now she was experiencing it after all these years.

Then there was Taimur, her constant companion, a loyal friend. She had met him several years ago, after a performance in the city. She had been instantly drawn to his amicability, his spontaneity. He had complimented her on her art. 'I loved your performance this evening. Please invite me when you perform next. I am a lover of classical dance and am on the look-out for performances staged in the city.' He had invited her on a date with his typical natural flair. She was at ease with him and found the conversation titillating, but not frivolous. One could never be bored with such a man, with his quick repartees and jocular manner. It was the beginning of a long-standing friendship that remained steady over the years. A smile lingered on her face as she murmured softly, 'He's unlike most men I have met, having a unique quality - a kind of purity.' He was a well-groomed guy, did not take unwanted liberties and kept a decent distance. She yawned, finally deciding not to fight the fatigue, and shut her eyes.

She felt she had barely slept but it was morning when the phone rang again. It was Taimur. 'Look, have you read the papers today? Your performance of yesterday has drawn headlines. They say there is none like you. I am forced to congratulate you.'

She heard a low chuckle at the other end. As always, though he was concerned for her, his tone was flippant.

'I didn't know you could be forced to do anything, sir,' she retorted, trying to sound irritated but miserably failed.

'Anyway, if you are available tonight, we can celebrate. But the dinner will be on me.'

Roused into a lighter mood, Sangeeta agreed instantly. As she put down the phone, the maid entered with her breakfast tray with scrambled eggs and cereal and a steaming pot of black tea. The morning paper was laid on one side. She snatched it and searched excitedly for her name.

'*The enchantress enchants again,*' was written in bold letters right at the top of the Arts and Media page. A wave of triumph tingled her spine.

In the mornings Sangeeta followed an intense regimen, practicing her craft. Her evenings were spent at concerts where friends and fans thronged, and then stayed at parties into the late hours. But tonight, she looked forward to her dinner with Taimur.

She stood for a long time in front of her wardrobe filled with glamorous, brightly coloured outfits. Today she selected a simple black dress, neither bold nor subdued, not wanting to detract from her own beauty. She wanted to be herself, nothing more, nothing less.

Sangeeta was fifteen minutes late. As she casually entered Costa Nostra café, she saw Taimur waiting patiently at a table in a corner. As she approached, he looked up and smiled.

'Finally! I thought you were going to ditch me tonight, Ma'am,' Taimur said in a cheeky tone. As he rose to greet her, his eyes opened wide in admiration, she looked truly stunning in a flowing black dress that she carried with grace.

'Well, I'm here,' she said, taking in his admiring glance with satisfaction. There were few men in this segregated society with the skill to flatter women, admiring their feminism without making vulgar overtures. 'What a lovely place you have chosen. I love the ambiance. It is quiet and secluded, giving us ample space to connect in peace. I dislike restaurants with loud music which makes conversation impossible.'

'I agree,' Taimur replied, pleased.

The meal was sumptuous as expected. Taimur was a generous host. He remained silent, letting Sangeeta talk, complaining about her grueling schedule. 'Mohan Sahib needs to be more realistic. At least have a week in between concerts… And that Hina…'

Taimur nodded, watching her closely as she voiced her anxieties. Was she aware of what he was going to say to her tonight? He didn't think so - she was a naïve woman in many ways. Swarmed by fans, living in the lap of luxury, she was in a cocoon. She never came out of herself, or felt the pain of reality with its layers of complexity. She lived life on a day to day basis, accepting accolades and fame and unmindful of the future. She was like a child!

'Where are you?' Sangeeta waved her hand in his face, 'Are you going to sit and meditate forever? Come on, I am hungry.'

Taimur took a deep breath, 'Sangeeta, I want to tell you something, ask you for a favour.' There was a split-second pause. Sangeeta was puzzled. The next moment, a beautiful diamond and sapphire ring stared at her.

'Sangeeta, will you marry me?' The words rushed out of his mouth before his courage could fail him.

'What! Have you gone crazy? These are the last words I expected to hear tonight,' Sangeeta blurted, her look changed from puzzlement to anxiety, and finally to anger.

She waved her hand airily, 'I am in no mood for flirtation.'

'I am serious, Sangeeta. Your parents are dead, and I am forced to ask for your hand directly, rather than asking them as is the custom. It is time we both settled down.'

'Never! Never! Never!'

'Why, Sangeeta? Why?'

'I will not give up my career. I know if I marry you, I will have to leave it one day. That will be my death. I'd rather pay the supreme price of leading a single life to pursue a career with deep devotion.'

'You can have both, Sangeeta.'

'No! That is the lie men tell women. My mother was a great dancer, but she gave it all up when she married my father. He forbade her to dance and that was the day she died. I will not suffer her fate.'

'Don't be a fool and renounce the happiness you deserve in life.'

'Well, you have taken me by surprise. I thought you were not the marrying type and preferred friendship, not a solid commitment.'

'I must say you underestimated me. Every bachelor calls it a day and needs to settle down, raise a family and pursue a career seriously.'

'Then what will become of my career? You know how committed I am.'

'There is no stopping you from continuing your career.'

'How lightly you say this! Most men do not want their wives to work, but only manage households and raise children.'

'Well, firstly I am not that kind of man. And if you are determined to weigh everything inside out, you will never take a decision. I am sorely disappointed in you. I had no idea artists were so unromantic. In life you can't have all your answers boxed and fitted into one compartment, and artists, more nuanced than ordinary people, know better than that.'

'Are you telling me I should make a decision on sheer impulse that I may live to regret?'

Taimur sensed this was her final answer. He could not bear the pain of wasting his life and hanging like a loser around the woman he loved. He had to make up his mind one way or another. To protect himself from getting hurt he said, 'Come on, let's go, we are wasting our time.' He stood up.

Sangeeta looked crestfallen, hurt obvious on her face. 'You are no different from other men. You can't be friends with a woman. You plunge ahead mindlessly, pursuing your passion and hunger. Whether you know it or not, you have selfishly hurt me today!'

'All I know is, if someone cannot come to a timely decision, it goes into cold storage. And that is the end of it! Sorry to end the night this way, but I have to go now. Goodnight.'

As Taimur walked away, Sangeeta stared blankly at him. It didn't strike her that this was the last time she would set eyes on him. As the door closed behind him, her gaze fell to the ring he had left on the table. Instinctively, she wanted to call out but was unable to do so. It was getting late. She got up, fatigue seeping into her bones. She wished it could have ended differently. Fear of losing him engulfed her.

Sangeeta and Taimur didn't contact each other. Many months, dozens of concerts, a hundred or so parties later, Sangeeta heard through the grapevine that Taimur had got married to a girl in America, the land of opportunity, where everyone flocked these days. They said the girl was pretty, bearing an uncanny resemblance to Sangeeta. When the news reached Sangeeta, she feigned happiness she was far from feeling.

There were now two constants in Sangeeta's life: her loneliness, and the second, a certain diamond and sapphire ring that she wore every waking moment of her life. No one knew why.

A STRANGE BLOOD BOND

She had killed her sister in cold blood! Mira gasped at her sister's dead body lying inert on a charpoy. Her bony frame hung limply in a grotesque manner, her face was bloated, blood caked on her face. Momentarily she cowered, and then pulled herself up to salvage her composure. In the mirror she saw her haggard face mocking her. Next to her stood her accomplice, her brother, a crazy sneer on his face.

Mira knew she must contain herself, put on a mask of a bereaved woman traumatised by the death of her blood sister. Her eyes were blood-shot with no tears in them. She was holding back an intense emotion, but it was neither grief nor remorse. But from now on her pretense was her reality, reassuring sisterly grief to all.

After all those long years of wrangling and cursing between the two sisters, she had enacted the deed. They had brawled like angry chickens in their pen. Cloistered in one small house with very little natural light, they were suffocating and resorted to tearing each other apart. Their choices were few.

There was only one other person in their lives, their brother, Hamza. They both adored him to distraction, being the only man in their lives they held on to him tightly. He lived in his own space and to his mind his sisters were a millstone around his neck. He tolerated them like some necessary evil. His power was mighty like a sword, and he oiled and greased it till the oil dripped everywhere, soiling the ground. As far as he was concerned, his deeds were never wrong and he did not spend time over-thinking them. He had discarded thinking ages ago, as if it was unnecessary. He saw his two sisters, their faces contorted with rage, and the more he saw them in this state, the less he actually thought about them. And if he did, he dismissed it with a loud invective, 'Such puerile women! Fighting with each other like two cats!'

It was inevitable, therefore, that they morphed into crazy witches over time. They had brought this on themselves. Fate had not dealt badly with them - they were born in an upper middle-class family, but they had let many a chance slip away irretrievably.

Meena had been a talented young woman with entrepreneurial skills. Setting up the first boutique in town run by a woman, she quickly gained repute. A stream of women of all ages lined up to purchase garments from her. Every design was unique, customised to suit the tastes of her clients. She would tell them, 'I designed this especially for you, to match your personality and of course your body.' Because of this special treatment, the clients never went anywhere else. Meena remained a modest woman, who lived within her financial limits which were sometimes constrained. 'I believe in less production, but I will never compromise on quality.' Time was on her side, and with little competition, her business was booming.

Meena was a smart girl who knew her growing position in society. She had had a reasonable number of suitors, men enamoured by her business skills, but under some pretext or the other, she turned them down. When a young man with a slick tongue proposed to her, she snarled and told her brother, 'I will never wash his dirty clothes!' After another proposal she vehemently said, 'I can't stand him, who knows his underwear might smell!' Another time she denigrated a suitor who was masochistic and carried himself like a prince, 'He might be a crude fellow who probably picks his nose.' With these trepidations and fears, the years slid by, and she grew into an old woman. Age is ruthless to some people, and with Meena it turned her into a decrepit woman with a haggard frame, flat-chest and graying, dry straggly hair.

Age was no kinder to Mira either. She was squeezed into a small, twisted frame. Her hands and feet curled into unshapely form with the debilitating onset of arthritis. She remained single by choice, inconspicuous enough not to be noticed by potential suitors. She turned into an irascible woman with suppressed rage. She had once been scorned by a man she loved and consequently turned her rage on all men saying, 'All men are beasts, with beastly faces and beastly hearts.' Subsequently she closed that chapter of her life forever. She discarded all desire to dress well and ended up looking like a sun-soaked dried raisin.

With time the patronage of their brother, Hamza, was drying up and the household fell upon hard times. Confiding to a friend, who was his only confidante, he disclosed his dwindling interest returns. 'I am an unfortunate man, whatever I invest in ultimately becomes a black hole. Whatever stocks I buy drop every time the economy gets a jolt.' Hamza hunched his shoulders, cutting a sorry figure, 'If it was me alone, I could have borne it, but with two extra mouths to feed it is very difficult. And when I return home, I see them fighting like witches. There is no peace in my house. But for Mira I have a special corner in my heart. She is a born giver and caretaker.' More than anything in the world he yearned for peace. 'The problem is with my sister Meena. She has grown senile and fights like a witch all day. I don't know how long I can put up with her tantrums since I don't have a strong heart.' He lapsed into a deep brooding mood, his face dark and angry.

A few days later, it was raining heavily and the occupants of the house stayed indoors. They had sat down to a meagre meal and the mood was sombre. Suddenly Meena started to wail in loud lamentations, cursing her sister and brother for their neglect of her. She pointed an accusing finger at them, 'You starve me daily, as if you want to get rid of me. Mira gives me such small portions of food that it seems like she wants me to wither away. I will expose you to the whole world!' With those words her cries became louder.

All of a sudden, a spectral gloom filled the room. Mira, with all the strength she could muster, pulled her up and shoved her into the bedroom locking the door from outside. Meena continued wailing for a long time, until exhausted, her cries subsided.

A week passed and Mira and her brother listened to the anguished cries of their sister. Their hearts had hardened and they had no pity for her. After a few days, when they could hear no sound from the room, they finally opened the door. Meena was lying crumpled up on her bed, stone dead, with blood crusting on her face. They muffled their faces, the stink inside was unbearable.

They waited for nightfall. Under cover of darkness, Mira and Hamza wrapped their sister in a shroud without washing her dead body, drove to the nearby graveyard and lowered her into the ground. Afterwards they slunk back into their dark house where only a small bulb burnt, so that the neighbours would not suspect any wrongdoing. The following day, news was circulated in the vicinity that Meena had been taken ill and died. Neighbours gossiped and questions were raised but, as was customary, people's attention was erratic, their memory short-lived and the matter soon died down.

A STRANGE ENCOUNTER

Hawke's Bay beach stretched out to salute the green, frothing Arabian Sea. Its smooth, sandy shore was mottled with black rocks and clumps of straggly dried shrubs. Crowds of people thronged the place - couples strolling, kids swimming in the water and families in private groups picnicking on the beach. Just an hour away, amidst the hustle bustle of Karachi, these same people would have been different - they would perhaps be arguing about intrusive in-laws, their children would be quarrelling and families fretting over inflated household expenses. But away from the din of the city, in this calming and therapeutic sanctuary, they could discard the pressures and tensions of daily life and soothe their spirits.

Ali lay on the beach watching the crowds and letting the sand sift through his fingers. 'If only memories could be sifted this easily,' he thought.

His wallet lay open on his stomach revealing a photograph of a young girl with a delicate smile, bright large eyes and flowing black hair that added vibrancy to her otherwise fragile frame. This had been his fiancée - his recently deceased fiancée. He held the photograph up and stared at it blankly, expressionless. He had not shed a single tear in the last month. But each time he looked at the picture, something broke inside and he had to hold back a flood of tears building up like a tsunami within. Ah! It had been this very monster, the Arabian Sea, that had swallowed her in a flash!

He recalled a beautiful day, with radiant sunbeams slanting down, when he and Umbar drove down for the weekend. They were intoxicated with joy, especially when he put the engagement ring on her long, slender finger. How she twirled it proudly, kissing him on the cheek.

The afternoon tide was tumultuous, rising ogre-like from the depths. Umbar was a bold and fearless woman, given to impulsive acts. Wearing a pale green swimsuit, she ran into the waters and he ran in after her. She swam into deeper waters, defying the surging tide. Unable to catch up with her, he watched from a distance as a huge wave gathered momentum. He screamed, 'Come back, Umbar! Come back! The waves are too high!' She did not heed him, playfully beckoning him to follow. All at once a treacherous and mighty wave came crashing down and Umbar vanished from sight! Ali's body froze. He shouted for help, but there was no one in sight. In that instant he knew if he leapt forward, he too would be consumed by the monstrous sea. He struggled back to shore, dizzily stumbling out of the water. Her body was never recovered.

He couldn't summon the courage to come to this spot again. He couldn't bear the heartache and the remorse. Guilt suffocated him, adding to his misery. He was unable to save her that day and the thought paralysed him. He had to reckon with his inner ghosts, whether it was sheer cowardice or plain caution that stopped him from going ahead to save her.

Today, after a year, he had forced himself to return. Perhaps it would help him in some way to relive the moment. The relentless ocean stretched ahead for miles, emerald coloured, its waves foaming like racing horses, white manes swishing in the air. Could he simply throw memories into its vast body, to drift away for good? The ocean was cruel. No matter how far memories are flung, the waves bring them back to this shore, more painful and weightier, like a dead body.

He desperately needed a swim and plunged into the warm water, feeling his body give in to a restive calm. The tide was low and the waves friendly and lulling. He tired after a while, dried himself with a towel and strolled on the rocky beach. The cool wind was refreshing and clean, unlike the city air.

Then he saw the girl!

She was on the beach, conspicuous in a green swimsuit. She shaded her eyes from the glaring sunlight as the water lapped at her bare legs. Barely a few yards away, she did not notice him at first. Instinctively, as if she felt his eyes piercing her back, she turned slowly to face him and momentarily she started.

Their eyes met and remained fixed until she turned back towards the sea. Normally he was not open to strangers, but this girl attracted him. He cleared his throat and said, ‘Hello… I’m Ali.’

She turned and smiled an engaging smile, ‘I’m Sara.’

‘What a lovely day it is!’ and then very casually, ‘Are you here by yourself or with friends?’ hoping he did not sound intrusive.

'Yes, I'm on my own! I'm an artist and we artists don't really need company. Give us a brush, a palette of paints and a location like this. And that's all we need,' she said smiling broadly. And then turning towards the sea, she added, 'I just love the ocean! Isn't it mesmerising?' She took a deep breath, flinging her hair back, the wind audaciously playing with her wavy locks. Turning back towards Ali, she asked 'And you? Let me guess…you're a banker?'

'Yes, how did you guess?' Ali asked, a hint of surprise in his tone.

'We artists are known to have shrewd eyes, but it doesn't take much to identify a banker from a mile away,' Sara said playfully, as Ali blushed pink. 'They all have a "we know it all" air about them.'

'Oh, really!' Ali laughed lightly. 'I never really thought about it. You are a discerning person!'

'Oh, that is part of the creative process, tossing things upside down, plucking out the kernel and building anew. Actually, I have faith in my gut feeling, it never betrays me,' she said gaily, taking a quick liking to this stranger.

She kept up a stream of chatter, uncomfortable with the silence that normally stands between two strangers. 'Anyway, I love this beach, this vast ocean which is a symbol of great strength. It's near the city, but induces serenity in the midst of its turbulence. You know nature doesn't intrude on our privacy like people do.'

Whilst they talked Sara had not stood still, constantly pacing like a restive spirit. There was vibrant energy in her slim, brown body as her muscles flexed. She seemed vaguely familiar, or was imagination playing tricks with his mind.

Stopping suddenly, she cried, 'Oh I am ravenous! I guess it's the crisp, fresh air that is making me hungry.' She laughed and started walking towards her hut. 'Yes, me too,' Ali added, as he followed her in the same direction.

As Sara walked towards her hut Ali called out, 'Surprise, surprise! Your hut is just next to mine!' After a pause, he added, 'Hey, why don't we share whatever we have, then we can eat together.'

He was a trifle embarrassed by his bluntness, but relieved by her response, 'Oh yes! That should add some spice to the meal, more variety as well.'

They brought their food baskets, unpacked, and spread out a delicious array of salads, meats and sandwiches. There was silence whilst they ate. Intrigued by the girl, Ali watched her with a sidelong look. There was something about her that resembled Umbar, not her looks, but something in her mannerism, the way she walked and talked. Her spirited manner too rang a bell somewhere in his mind.

'And your family?' he asked, touching a chord inside her.

Sara turned away momentarily, staring ahead, then looked at Ali, talking candidly, 'If you want to know the whole story, my parents are both dead, they died in a road accident when I was in my teens. Since then I've been on my own, hopping from one aunt's place to another, struggling to make a living.' She paused awhile as she ate, then added with a touch of sadness, 'I guess it isn't easy here without parental support, especially if you are striving to become an artist.' She looked at him with an engaging smile, 'But things have eased out over time, and I have managed to make things work for myself. I have my independence and I love it! This is the crux of my life. And now you tell your story.'

'Well, I keep long hours with little time for play. I am presently living alone in the city. But let's see how long I stay here - I'm thinking of moving,' Ali said, looking away at the ocean, knowing well he had chosen not to say what was, perhaps, a crossroad in his life, a kind of escape. What had motivated him was buried somewhere deep in his wallet. An aching pain rumbled through his body.

'Why would you move?' she exclaimed. 'I love this city. You know it has energy, like no other city in the country. Of course, things were better before, but that's life you know, with its ups and downs. Still, I have great faith in our shared humanity, our ability to swing back in the midst of the tremendous baggage this city carries in its underbelly. There is inexplicable crime and violence that erupts all the time - dividing decent folks like us and the criminal elements'

'Yes, I fear things are not changing the way we want them to. Look at Karachi, in a matter of a few years it has transitioned from a hub of many peace-loving ethnicities to a city ripped apart with strife. Tolerance for each other's differences has declined to zero. People get killed on a daily basis and nothing makes sense anymore.' Ali spoke poignantly, 'Human life has lost its value.'

Meanwhile Sara paced restlessly, her brow furrowed. The young man had compassion. She liked sensitive men - it showed a higher intellect, more polish. Her heart skipped a beat and she recalled her own situation a few years ago. Aloud she said, 'There are memories bottled up inside both of us, let's not dwell on them for too long.'

'A dear one lost?' he enquired, seeing sadness on her face.

'A close friend,' she replied with resigned sigh. 'He was caught in a crossfire between two rebel groups.'

'Oh, I'm sorry,' was all he could muster, as a familiar bell rang.

'Don't be sorry. I'm sure he's happy, wherever he is, and that's all that matters,' Sara replied, a strange smile on her face.

She is a weird girl, Ali thought. She conceals her loss with composure. Cool indeed! Positivity is admirable. This girl has depth that perhaps surfaces only in her artistic creations.

Now he had heard her story, could he reveal his story to her? No! His wound was too raw and could not be touched. It could spoil on exposure. He couldn't handle it for the time being. Perhaps over time he would be able to face it better. He turned his eyes on her. He liked her self-assurance, her straight posture and her black hair blowing in the wind. Even in sadness she looked charming, her windswept hair giving her a wild look. Oh, how he would love to play with that hair, twist the strands around with his fingers and tell her they shared a common grief. His mind was wandering. He moved a step back to keep a distance.

Reading his thoughts and wishing them away, she started 'Oh, I am feeling the heat so much! I am going into the sea for a swim.' He watched her step into the water, her hands gently dipped in, feeling the tempo of the waves, before she plunged in. She took bold, confident strokes. It was exhilarating to get away from the humid, sultry air of the city.

The sun was setting, mixing its iridescent colours in the water, as lamps were being turned on in the huts along the shore. The roar of the sea was getting louder, sounding like a raging monster. In the faraway distance, the sky and sea met in one line, embracing like lovers. Sara emerged from the water and strolled towards her hut.

Ali remained on the beach, hesitating to go into his hut as it would be warm inside. His limbs were tired and languid. The saline water had sucked the soreness from his body and now it rested supine, like a limp rag. His eyelids struggled to remain open.

Suddenly he was roused from deep slumber. He heard a sound, then his eyes fell on a figure, faraway on the beach. It was a girl, walking slowly into the water, a long, slim, brown figure, a body glistening in the fading light. Slowly she entered the water, gracefully like a nymph.

She looked like a creature of the sea, ethereal, shimmering, moonlight cascading on her naked body. It revealed her silhouette before she disappeared into the water, a silvery hue, as the ocean sucked her into its voracious belly.

An anguished cry escaped his lips and his body shook uncontrollably. He was bathed in sweat. There was an unstoppable urge to run towards her, rescue her, drag her back on shore. But his body was stiff like a corpse, paralysed. His mind worked feverishly. He couldn't lose her again; his wounds had not yet healed. He thrashed his limbs like a frightened animal.

He was woken by sunlight blazing down on him. He was on the beach. The events of the previous night resonated in his mind. Was it a dream, a memory which even today, threw him into a paroxysm of misery? He was conscious of a throbbing ache at the back of his head where it had rested on the sand.

He turned to her hut. He blinked in a circle of glaring sunlight to see the girl coming out, light-footed and sprightly. No tell-tale signs of the previous night. His mind squirmed. Questions haunted him but he could not articulate them. He knew she would laugh and think him crazy if he dared ask her.

'Hey, how are you today? I was just leaving. I'm almost done with my painting.'

'Hi, I will be taking off soon as well. Have to get back to work tomorrow.'

He lingered, hoping to have few more minutes, 'It was really nice meeting you.'

'It was good meeting you as well,' she smiled candidly looking into his eyes, holding them for a moment. She looked sun-burnt, ravished by fiery elements. Her eyes sparkled, more sea-green than ever, freshly dyed by seawaters.

Then, overcome, he knew he couldn't let her go. He must get to know her better, connect with her again. The anguish of his previous loss rose once again. He had to hold her somehow, keep her in his sight, he couldn't lose her.

Instinctively, he cried out, 'Stop! Why don't you stay longer?' She halted in her tracks, startled by his quivering voice. His face was distorted and his lower jaw twitched. Momentarily, she looked confused at this sudden overture. With a quick wave of her hand she called out, 'Sorry, I am running late, probably another time, another place,' and turned and climbed into her car. She threw back another glance, smiled weakly and started the car, and before he could blink, she was racing down the road, leaving a thick trail of sand behind.

His heart sank, for an excruciating moment he was rooted to the ground, staring stupidly at the empty space ahead. 'A very decent girl indeed,' he muttered under his breath. Then he turned and headed back to the beach, overcome with exhaustion. He slipped a hand into his pocket and retrieved his wallet. He removed the picture and on a sudden impulse was going to throw it into the water, when he took a deep breath and held back.

A moment, dark and surreal, whisked by like a turbulent cloud. He shook his head and placed the picture back into the wallet as tears welled in his eyes. This time he gave in to them and collapsed on the sandy beach, sobbing uncontrollably.

A STRANGE LOVE AFFAIR

The woman had fallen madly, passionately in love with the man. The man, whom she found to be very attractive, was middle-aged, years younger than her. She couldn't quite place what it was about him that lured her. It might have been the twinkle in his eye, or his impish and daring demeanour. She could not resist him. She admitted with candour that she daydreamed about love in all its purity. This was lacking in her ex-husband, who had been cold and distant during the many years they had been married. An older man, he could not satisfy a young woman like her who was intense and poetic, like a thirsty plant.

That cold sombre day she had gone to Alhambra to watch a play. The first time she saw him he was standing at the ticket counter and she stood in line behind him. He turned courteously towards her and offered her his spot so she could go before him. She declined politely. He read her face instantly, a woman of distinction, good family lineage, well composed and elegant in gait and carriage. Would she respond to his overture? He didn't think that he had been rebuffed, and simply got his ticket and walked into the theatre and took his seat. Ensconced in his chair with a mug of coffee, he sensed a movement, soft like eiderdown, and there she was, sinking into the seat next to him. Providence had strange ways of connecting people.

The play was a comedy show, awash with good humour, satirical and witty. Throughout the play she laughed hilariously and he guffawed, both sharing a sense of humour. During the intermission he shared a bag of popcorn with her that she happily accepted. There was vigour in her carriage, an enthusiasm for life that was infectious. He asked her, 'What are you doing tomorrow?' She replied instantly, 'Nothing in particular.' His next question was expected, 'Then why don't we meet up for coffee?' 'Oh yes!' was the prompt reply.

That started a chain of dates. They met frequently at coffee shops and later in hotels. They had plenty to talk about, soul-searching conversations about life's ebb and flow, and how it is navigated on a daily basis.

She told him of her life as a single person - she had a daughter who was the love of her life that a cold marriage of alienation had not spoiled. He told her he was married, yet unattached emotionally. He had a son who was the reason they stayed together. His wife's sour, slovenly disposition led to their falling out long ago. Yet the comfort of marriage held them together.

He told her, 'Men are polygamous by nature, yet societal bonds tie us down. I would have left her long ago if it was not for my cowardly soul. And then, I adore my son.' The woman liked his candour; he opened up like a book.

They were not afraid to expose their frayed emotions to each other. She looked at him with tear-filled eyes, hoping against hope for a lifetime union. There was an element of reckless love in their affair, though neither was young. The fear of being seen and exposed never crossed her mind, but it entered his mind, like a haunting nightmare.

Perhaps his stakes were higher than hers.

Time passed as the man and woman continued to feed off each other with love and adoration. He was an attentive listener and she shared her inner life. Her lonely life fed a needy desire to connect with him. She told him about her parents, her siblings, the trials of a single life and raising a child alone. She confided in him, 'The pain of raising a child is miniscule compared to the love and satisfaction that a mother gets. In this way, she learns to come out of her shell, embrace life, and become a giver.' He listened with intensity and could not have enough of her. 'It is true, we learn from our children and grow with them. Parenting and loving are humbling in many ways. You have humbled me in many, many ways, my love, and made me look inwards, without guilt or remorse. Guilt corrodes and is futile.'

She began to think by now that it might lead somewhere, to a certain kind of fruition. Her ideals fed her euphoria, did not diminish it. She had boundless energy to laugh, to flirt and to make love. There was not a boring moment with her. 'You are a breath of fresh air,' he told her gushingly. 'You have taught me to relish every moment spent with you.'

He himself was a practical man, a family man, with issues of diminishing funds that cut his enthusiasm sorely. His advertising business was dwindling and money was squeezed from all sides. His wife's extravagance and his own drinking addiction had piled debts on him. Life had turned into a mixed bag of anxiety and hope.

The man and woman continued to meet, blind to a storm brewing around them. They craved to live in the moment, take life as it comes. It was a play they acted out together. Blissful ecstasy held their nameless union. This play-acting was real sensually, albeit rootless. It was a floating fantasy, orbiting on wings of desire. It was surreal, more vibrant than conjugal unions that can drag on into a timeless void which begets rot.

She was free and riding on euphoria, wanting it all. He was a practical man as well, with family issues dragging him down. His wife was on his trail, having appointed spies to track him.

One day, on his way to visit the woman, they surrounded him, restrained him and dragged him home. He remained dysfunctional for days. His wife threatened exposure and divorce. She shouted, 'I will take the child with me, he cannot live with a father who has lost his mind!' She was from an influential family, and he knew she would be true to her word. He was plagued by a haunting fear of losing his son.

One cold morning, she waited for him at their usual time. He was always punctual so she became anxious as the minutes passed. She called his cell phone but it was powered off. Her anxiety increased. There was no other way she could contact him. As evening fell, she knew he would not come. Every day she waited to hear a light footstep at the door, an impatient ring of the bell, but there was silence.

By the fifth day she knew he would never come back. With a sinking heart, she conjured his image in her mind. This was not the way she expected it to end. After all the intimacy, love and passion, she expected a kinder farewell. She knew all along it would end, but not in this way. She was desperate for closure, a cushion to lay her dead wreath on.

The woman shook like a reed, memories swelled to the surface. There was an empty feeling inside her, of being hollowed out. Would her trust in the purity of love be forever broken, or would her dreams survive beyond the breakaway? She held up her head, her look meditative, her heart ripped like a defiled temple.

A WOMAN IN ECLIPSE

In the cloistered green suburban locality of Model Town was a mansion known as Shehzadi, a fitting name for its resident. It had lived up to its name in its heyday, when men and women alike flocked to enjoy its lavish parties and intellectual debates amongst the elite of the city. Those were the glorious days for the occupants of Shehzadi, when the lights were always on.

Now, years later, nostalgia hung in the air, as did a musty odour of dank, unventilated and abandoned rooms. As with other households in the Model Town locality of Lahore, a city of old wealth, fortune had passed from generation to generation, not earned but bequeathed, stagnant but still abundant, and like water that remains still, had turned to fungal-like rot.

Nestled in an exclusive niche, the mansion looked eerie and shadowy, as did its occupants, to the *naukars*, its servants, and also to those working in other homes in the neighbourhood. A group of *naukars* sat nearby under a banyan tree, chewing betel leaves and whiling away the afternoon. 'This is a strange household,' sighed Maqbool, the oldest man in the group. It was clear from his tone had he was the most knowledgeable in the group and had information about many of the households in the area.

'Who lives there?' asked Iqbal, a newcomer to the neighbourhood clique of servants, seeking to learn all the local gossip.

'A couple called Saira Bano and Saifullah with their two sons, Ahsan and Ahmad,' replied Maqbool. 'The house belonged to Begum Saira Bano's parents. Her father, Ehsanullah, was a wealthy businessman of his day, and his wife was a commanding woman of stature. Saira Bano was their only daughter, the apple of her father's eye whom he indulged excessively. Few fathers are more protective about their daughters. She was a beautiful girl, special in every way. When he died he left everything to her, enabling her to maintain a comfortable lifestyle.'

Then lowering his voice to share a secret, Maqbool whispered, 'Begum Saira Bano's children are from an earlier marriage with a man named Taimur. I always liked him. He was a well-bred gentleman, kept the *naukars* in the neighbourhood happy. He was generous and friendly, lived up to his status, *Mashallah*. I remember that the couple fought often. That's what their servant would tell me. Or I should say, servants, because they kept changing all the time. Then, one day he left. None of the servants could really tell why. However, they said Begum Saira Bano was not much affected. She hired an extra nanny to make sure that the children were well cared for and did not miss their father. And then a few years later, she married Saifullah Sahib. He's also a nice gentleman and is again very generous. He gave us generous gifts of money last Eid.'

After a minute's pause, choosing his words cautiously, Maqbool continued, 'But it's not like the old times when Ehsanullah Sahib used to live here. There is something missing. It's like a ship that was magnificent in its time, but is now drifting on the ocean, anchorless and lost.' Shaking his head, he said, 'I'm tired of this topic, we have discussed it to death. Who has heard the new Hadiqa Kiyani song? She sings well and looks pretty, much better than the Bollywood heroines.'

A short distance away, inside the drawing room of her mansion, Saira Bano reclined on a plush velvet chair, pensively rocking back and forth. She looked like an artifact from a museum, perfectly carved, with large almond eyes heavily lined with eyeliner. Her profile defined an aquiline nose and a wide full mouth sporting bright red lipstick. It was the face of one of those ancient queens of Egypt whose exotic beauty and aura of romance still lingered, dust-laden, like folklore. She fitted aptly in her mansion, grandiosely decorated in Victorian style, its aging gaudy décor unchanged since her parents' death.

Saira Bano's eyes were fixed upon her father's portrait on the wall - a tall man and strongly built, with almond shaped eyes and an aquiline nose, like his daughter's. He had an aristocratic air, with a soft, gentle face and kind eyes.

The silence was interrupted when Saifullah stepped into the drawing room.

'Lost in your thoughts again, I see,' Saifullah said, making a concerted effort to bring cheer to an eerily silent room.

'Hmm,' Saira Bano mouthed tersely.

'Would you like to go to a musical concert at the Alhambra tonight? The renowned Nusrat Fateh Ali is performing. Come on, it'll be a nice change,' Saifullah said excitedly.

'Not really. This heat gets to me, it's exhausting. But here's tea. Have a cup, please,' Saira replied. Breathing a heavy sigh, she stood up from her chair and walked out of the room. 'I'm going to take a nap.'

Saifullah, undeterred, smiled faintly, his eyes following his beautiful wife as she walked gracefully from the room. He settled down in a chair, deep in thought. It had been fifteen years since their marriage. He loved her today as he had done since he first laid eyes on her, when he adored her from a distance, before they married.

In those days he would have given anything to sweep her off her feet. After all, she was beautiful and elegant, with a distinguished family background. People gossiped that he had married her to bolster his personal status. There was a grain of truth in it, but he did truly love her. She was Ehsanullah's beloved daughter, resembling him in looks, though perhaps not in traits and character. She lived in her own world and he respected her privacy, giving her the space she needed. She, on her part, gave him a reasonable measure of attention and respect, content as long as he was not intrusive in her private life. He knew she was spoilt and self-absorbed, selfish to the core, but he loved her all the same.

Unlike Saira Bano's first husband, Saifullah was not given to discontent, and also liked some independence in his marriage. He had his own circle of close friends. With a connoisseur's taste for good food and company, he entertained them lavishly, and they rallied to him. There was no dearth of finances, their coffers were full.

As Saifullah remained lost in thought, he heard footsteps. It was Nazeera, the maid, at the door. She looked visibly perturbed. 'Saifullah Sahib, do you know where I can find Ahsan Sahib? I was cleaning his rooms and it appears he hasn't been home for a few nights. I hope he's all right!'

Saifullah grew alarmed, 'He might be at a friend's place, but ask Ahmad. He would know.'

As Nazeera went off to find Ahmad, Saifullah leaned back uneasily in his chair, trying to quell the fear rising in his mind. He knew that his wife's sons, Ahsan and Ahmad, led lives independent of their mother. Accustomed to their mother's self-centredness, they had learned to rely on themselves. There was a close bond between them but they were poles apart in their tastes and temperament. Ahsan was shy and introverted, with few friends, and spent his time reading and listening to music. Ahmad was gregarious, restless and aggressive, with a large circle of friends with whom he hung out daily, often in the nocturnal hours. Yet the boys were strongly attached to each other, filling a vacuum in their lives.

Saifullah felt warm affection towards his stepsons, they were good boys but at the end of the day he knew they were not of his blood. If he was ever likely to forget, he was reminded of this by his wife. He remembered ruefully the day he had gently admonished her. 'I know you love the boys. But has it ever dawned on you that they need something more than love? They need a vibrant connection with their mother, a more hands-on support now that they are growing up. They need their parents to guide them, steer them towards higher ground, to be rooted in their reality.'

He had been rewarded with an icy stare from Saira. 'They are my boys. Not yours. Not their father's. They are mine.' From then onwards he had taken care to distance himself from the boys, but he did care for them and a relative harmony was thus maintained in the house, with each one of them going their separate ways.

A whole day passed and Ahsan was still missing. Saifullah hired men to search for him. Word circulated that Ahsan was last seen with a group of friends. Now panic filled the house. Saira Bano, for once, was forced out of her stupor, and gloom descended on the house. The following day, the family was awakened by screams in the early hours of morning. Saira Bano, hearing the commotion, rushed out. Saifullah followed her. 'I found the door of the annexe open,' yelled the guard. 'I went to check and this was what I found!'

'What has happened, for God's sake, somebody tell me,' Saira cried hysterically. She and Saifullah followed the guard to Ahsan's secluded annexe.

When she entered the room Saira stared wide-eyed, uttering a loud, terrified scream. There, in a pool of blood, was Ahsan's dead body. On the table there were half-empty glasses of wine. Chairs were scattered topsy-turvy in every direction. Apparently Ahsan had had company. He had come home sometime in the late hours with male company. What happened then was a mystery.

The room filled with the low wailing of Saira Bano who was clinging to the dead body of her son. She looked like a white spectre of death.

The news of Ahsan's death spread like wildfire. The air was rife with speculation and rumour-mongering. Some alleged wildly that Ahsan was involved with gangs dealing with narcotics. There was no proof of this and the family vehemently denied it. Saira Bano and Saifullah were tortured by these allegations and refused to meet anyone. The issue was compounded because they were clueless about Ahsan's friends and there was a total absence of trails leading to that night and the previous days. Ahsan's friends remained shrouded in mystery and the terrible enigma deepened.

The family belonged to a minority sect and had always lived in fear. In the following days the police carried out investigations and interrogated many people, but nothing came out of it and the case was eventually closed.

After the funeral Saira Bano went into quiet seclusion, confined to her room. Saifullah, knowing his wife, left her alone. Her grief was great and she was inconsolable. He felt helpless and insignificant, and kept a distance. A month passed and there were no signs of her emerging from her dark moods, and Saifullah was greatly disturbed. 'Saira Bano, what is the point of brooding all day?' Saira burst into tears, crying hysterically, 'I think of Ahsan constantly. He was a darling boy, very undemanding. I neglected him but he never rebelled. He continued to love me, was obedient and never misbehaved, even when we disagreed with each other.'

Saifullah held his wife in silence whilst she continued to weep. 'I was more attentive to Ahmad, because he is an extrovert with a loving nature. I suspected Ahsan was hurt by my partiality towards Ahmad. He was always a quiet child but became increasingly withdrawn over the years. Of late, he spent all his time in the seclusion of his rooms. Now he is dead and with him lies buried his lonely situation that consumed him all these years. I will never forgive myself.'

Saifullah knew what she said was closer to the truth than he liked to admit. 'Now, now! Don't cry, *merijan.*Shhh,' he consoled her, relieved that Saira was expressing her emotions. Venting her grief would do her good.

When Saira Bano eventually emerged after six months of self-imposed mourning, she looked pale and haggard. She turned to Ahmad for consolation, but did not find it. Ahmad was cold and looked desolate, having grieved over his brother's death alone. Saira Bano was consumed with self-pity. She had lost both her sons, one had died and now the other was estranged. Emerging from her cocoon, tortured and hurt, the new reality of her flawed relationship with her son gnawed at her, like a knife cutting into her skin.

One day as she lay in her dark, unlit room, chasing the ghosts of her mind, Ahmad came to see her. 'Mother, I am leaving today,' he said, his voice distant, mechanical, as if he had rehearsed these words many times. Saira Bano looked at him dumbfounded. 'Where are you going, sweetheart?'

'I am going to America to join my father. He has sent for me. I know my future is in that country with him,' Ahmad replied coldly. Saira Bano frowned. 'Where has this sudden love between father and son come from after so many years? Didn't he betray you by leaving when you both were young, leaving me alone to raise you? You know how difficult it has been.'

Staring straight into his mother's eyes, Ahmad said, 'He left to protect us from your battles. But the question is, were you ever with us?'

'Are you questioning my love?' Saira Bano asked in a quivering voice.

'I am not questioning your love. But did it ever occur to you that Ahsan and I needed something more than motherly love?' Ahmad replied.

Saira Bano took a deep breath. She had heard this before from both her husbands, but somehow, hearing it from her son left her speechless.

There was a moment of silence before she uttered in a quivering voice, 'What will become of me? Have you given it any thought? I have lost one son, and now I will be losing the other. Have a heart, son, why are you forsaking me at this point in my life?'

'Mother, you have Mr Saifullah. He has always given you unfaltering support.'

Her heart was sinking. Like one who knows that the end is near, she made one desperate attempt to hold him back. 'Ahmad, I want you here with me. I cannot live without you! I command you to stay! I will die without you!'

'Mother, it is too late. Nothing can hold me back. I am leaving.' Ahmad desperately wanted to end this conversation before he said anything he would later regret. He stepped forward and hugged his mother, kissed her lightly on the cheek and quickly withdrew. Just before he left he looked back momentarily, for the last time, at the woman who had always haunted him in his dreams. He had loved, admired and hated her all at the same time.

Years later, on a hot, sunny afternoon, a group of neighbourhood servants were sitting under the banyan tree as usual. The air was unusually sultry. Conversation drifted to the occupants of Shehzadi. A newcomer to the group asked who lived in the mansion. The old *naukar*, Maqbool replied, 'There is a lady by the name of Saira Bano who lives there alone. Her husband passed away a year ago. One son was murdered and the other left for a foreign land, never to return. That's life for you, harsh and brutal!' Then with a faraway look in his eyes, he added, 'I always compared this mansion to an anchorless ship. Now the captain is left alone on a once-magnificent ship.'

A short distance away Saira Bano sat in her drawing room with curtains drawn to prevent the bright sunlight from entering. She stared blankly at the portrait of her father, Ehsanullah. This was the one man who had never disappointed her. The rest either died or went away or could not live up to her expectations, unable to give her the love her father had showered on his beloved daughter.

In the background on an old television set a young lady was quoting Mark Twain. 'The past is a regret, the future an experiment.' Saira Bano did not pay attention to these words as she continued to stare at her father's portrait. After all, for some people who live in the past, the present is static and the future quite predictable.

A WOMAN OF LEISURE

The woman lit a cigarette and with slow deliberation puffed on it, blowing out the dense, swirling smoke from her puckered lips. She lounged idly on a comfortable pink couch where she usually spent her days. She was a woman of leisure with an abundance of inherited wealth, cocooned in a world of her own making. Women of her class had the privilege to construct and deconstruct their lives to fit any style of living that suited them.

The doorbell rang and she walked mechanically to open the door. It was the man who had been courting her for months. Her heart beat faster as he walked in with a confident stride. He was a man of medium height, balding and with twinkling eyes set in a round face. He was older than she was, but sprightly. 'Hello my dear! I was missing you, so I thought I would come and see you. You haven't answered any of my calls!'

'I'm sorry, I didn't mean to be rude, but I was unwell,' she replied, avoiding his gaze.

'Are you sure you are not avoiding me? You know I love you with all my heart and I want to marry you. If you just say "Yes" you will make me the happiest man in the world!' he exclaimed.

She paled at his words, and then she spoke quickly, afraid that if she did not speak now she might lose her words forever. 'You know that it is not possible, even if I want to. You do not have a job. You live with your brother on his farm. How do you think we will sustain ourselves? My brothers will not let me continue to live in this family house and nor will they keep on supporting me once we get married. Please understand my dilemma.' Her voice quivered but she held back her tears.

The man winced as if slapped in the face. 'If this is what you think then my chances are slim. I should take my leave.' He rose slowly and walked towards the door.

She looked at him sadly. 'I'm sorry I've hurt you. It was not my intention.'

He shook his head and said, 'Never mind, words once uttered cannot be taken back, but you spoke your truth.' Having said this, he left. She stood on the curved veranda watching his car as it disappeared from sight. Before turning the corner, he glanced back to capture her image one last time. He knew he wouldn't see her again.

She went back into the room and sat on the couch. As she switched on the television, the room echoed with loud music and her spirit calmed. She called out to her old and loyal servant, 'Please bring me my tea.'

'Yes memsahib,' was the prompt reply and she was served steaming hot tea in a delicate china cup. She sipped the tea pensively as she slowly composed herself.

She was in the habit of doing things her way, confined to her immense derelict house that had all the trappings of an earlier and prosperous age. It stood back at a dignified distance from a once busy main street, seemingly forgotten by the world. Its colonial architecture was still imposing, with a curved veranda held up by solid pillars, high ceilings and heavy unpolished, carved wooden doors. It was furnished in an archaic style with now shabby sofas and photographs of a family that had once been in the upper echelons of power during the British Raj, looking down arrogantly from the walls. The walls of this house with their peeling paint stood stoically. They held her together so she would not fall apart. This brick and mortar gave her more strength than the pleasure of love and intimacy with all its possibilities. She had never liked the smell of fresh paint for it was strange and unfamiliar, like a foreign language. She could live within these walls forever and when she died her ghost would, until eternity, haunt this place.

The youngest sibling in a family of eight, she was her father's pet, and as a child she would sit on his lap whilst he sang her lullabies and told her stories of fairy princesses who lived in faraway castles and were invariably rescued by a prince in shining armour. 'My little princess,' he would murmur in her ear and his chubby darling would put her little hands around him and feel his warm comforting body. When she became too big to sit on his lap he would sit her beside him and tell her stories based more on fantasy than reality. The stories that particularly stayed with her above all others were stories of the doomed love of Romeo and Juliet, lovers unable to marry, and love that ended tragically. The young girl was stricken by these sad stories that left a deep impression on her. When her father died not long after, his precious daughter was left in limbo.

Her mother was left alone to raise a large family and could not give each one the special attention they needed. The youngest lived on the periphery, isolated and lonely. Her brothers treated her like a baby and for her sisters, she was the doll they played with. She saw all this with her wide innocent eyes and her soft heart.

With time, her siblings married and left home. Her brothers courted independent-minded girls and went on to marry one by one. Her sisters found well-to-do boys and joyfully tied the marital knot. The nest was virtually empty. The young woman and her mother sat together all day long as the days went by, the sun rising and setting, the passing of different seasons, and they sat as if nothing had changed. Together they watched television and listened to love songs to fill their lives with a bit of romance.

Eventually her mother passed on, her aging soul reposing in her final abode, and the woman was left alone in the big lonely house. She was not prepared for this new situation. She faced it all with a childlike innocence, taking each day as it came.

The years went by but she stood static like a question mark with no answer. Then she met this man, a strange one at that, who wanted to marry her, but he was hanging like a kite without a string, with nowhere to go and no place to stay. She knew if she married him there would be two kites without strings instead of one.

The telephone rang and she rose stiffly. It was the man again who refused to give up on her. A delicious tingle went down her spine - she liked being pursued. 'Hello dear! I just rang to ask how you were?' the caller said in a low tone.

'I am fine! How are you, dear?' she said simply. 'Thank you for ringing up.'

There was a pause at the other end, the caller was waiting for a more welcoming, less tepid response, and not receiving one, he hung up. After she put the phone down she smiled to herself, 'He refuses to give up on me and probably finds me irresistible.'

Suddenly she remembered she must ring up her sister. It was a brief conversation. 'How are you?' she asked.

'I'm okay, just a lingering ache from arthritis which won't go away,' responded her sister.

'Oh, so sorry to hear that,' she replied. 'I will pray you feel better. By the way, he called yesterday.'

There was a pause at the other end. 'What did he say?' asked the sister curiously.

'Oh, nothing really, the same old thing,' she answered cautiously. 'I will talk to you again tomorrow. Goodbye!' That was it, nothing more, nothing less, for there was nothing further to be said.

She had slowly stopped sharing her innermost thoughts and feelings with others, unable to share a part of herself with anyone, and had, in the process, become a stranger to herself.

One day an old friend called, wanting to visit her. The woman was excited and went around the house announcing to the servants that a visitor was expected. She searched her wardrobe for something decent to wear. Then she saw the dress, the one she had worn to a former boyfriend's party thirty years ago. She remembered the day as if it was yesterday. If only he had proposed that day, as she had desperately wanted. It would have changed everything. She pressed her face into the dress which smelled of faded perfume and something stirred within her. She returned to the closet and chose a simple dress. She looked critically at herself in the mirror. Her eyes were puffy with dark shadows, her face drawn as if someone had stretched her skin downwards. She barely recognised herself, 'I look much older than I feel,' she murmured. She rubbed some rouge on her cheeks, hoping to reduce the pallor.

Finally, the friend arrived. The two embraced warmly. 'It's been so long since we met! Where have you been? Why haven't you been in touch?' the friend cried excitedly.

The friend was astute, worldly-wise, and in a flash took in everything. She had brought a box, carefully wrapped with ribbon. 'I have brought you these chocolate cookies. I remember you always liked them.'

The woman opened the box and helped herself to the cookies, remembering to offer some to her friend. The visitor looked on as if nothing was amiss, and when the servant brought in the tea, she took it politely saying, 'Thank you.'

Her eyes lingered for a moment on the bowing servant, as if waiting for him to say something. But he only lowered his head and left the room. She looked at her friend, smiling innocently and shrugged her shoulders. She empathized with her complicated situation, living in utter solitude, surrounded by servants who served her, yet nothing could mitigate her distress.

An hour elapsed and a one-sided discourse ensued between the two during which the friend talked ceaselessly to fill the silence. 'Oh, Sabrina asked about you and I scolded her and asked why she had not called you. My ex-husband would always say that old friends are gold, they never rust or show age. One can always catch up with them at any point in your life. They are like a tough thread that will not snap.' Then she paused, and not getting a response except a dry smile, she went on doggedly, 'You know old pals are like closets where you can bury all your woes and they still remain concealed.'

There was still no light flickering in her friend's eyes, but she refused to give up, 'You must come to one of our regular parties that our group of friends take turns to host. We share a lot with each other, our literary and social activities, as well as our works of charity. It helps to pass the time, you know. Our nests are empty, our children have left, and days are monotonous. It will be good for you to get out,' she added. All the while the other woman listened quietly, passively, without responding. Then giving up, the friend took her leave whilst the woman stood in the veranda till the car disappeared from sight.

Then one day, not long after the friend's visit, there was a phone call. The bell kept ringing and today she did not have the energy to pick it up. The caller was unrelenting and bent on not giving up. Finally, she mustered the will to answer. It was her man! Her heart missed a beat. His voice was unusually vibrant. 'How are you? I have good news that I wanted to share with you. I got married last week,' he uttered in one long breathless voice. Her heart plummeted! There was a long pause at her end. 'Well, aren't you going to wish me well?' he sounded anxious. She forced herself to say, 'I'm very happy for you and wish you well.' He went on, 'Remember me in your prayers.'

'I will remember you in my prayers forever and always,' she said softly. She hung up quickly, but not before he heard her voice break. She returned to her couch, her familiar refuge in the living room, this time a trifle hurriedly. She sat down and started switching channels on the television. Soon she gave up and irritably threw the remote into a corner. Somewhere inside her welled a flood of helpless tears, full of remorse and fear of an uncertain future.

AFTER FIFTY LONG YEARS

He had waited patiently for her for fifty long years. He loved her with an intensity that was almost unique in its consistency. Perhaps she didn't love him in the same way, he didn't know. Many seasons had come and gone, and he continued to wait for her. He was a bystander when at the age of twenty she married another man, he remained a bystander when she bore children, and he was still a bystander when her husband contracted an illness and died, leaving her alone in a hostile world. During those long years he had continued to remain like any bystander on a sidewalk, unnoticed by passers-by.

When his beloved's husband died he lost no time in offering marriage to her, but his proposal was turned down, making him feel like a beggar seeking alms on a roadside. It was not that he was not eligible, it had nothing to do with that. It was not that he did not have a lucrative job, or that his family was not distinguished enough, or that he was not good looking. It was simply that she considered it an act of impropriety that he should ask for her hand in marriage when her husband had died so recently and she was still mourning him.

And years later, when he proposed after a great length of time, when he considered it appropriate, it was turned down because she said that the children were growing up and the entry of another man in the family would disrupt the household. And after many more years had passed, when he again asked for her hand in marriage, she replied simply, 'It is time for me to get my children married and not myself!'

When another few years went by and he again asked her hand in marriage, she replied, 'My married children will be embarrassed to see their mother marry a man for love at this age.' Undeterred, he kept waiting, not in a queue lined up with suitors, but a solitary man, not yet ready to bury his only love. He began to think it was a love unrequited that had lain for fifty years, living proof that love could burn audaciously alone without a flint to light it.

Then one day he received a call from her. He dared not hope, so asked nervously, 'Thank you for calling. What have I done to be worthy of receiving a call from you?' There was a pause at the other end, the caller was weighing her words before she answered. 'I am finally ready. It has been a long haul and I am tired to my bones. I deserve some happiness for myself and cannot be put on the cross any longer. Life passes by too quickly, and there are moments we are compelled to catch before they forsake us forever. I lost my husband and I suffered. I sacrificed for my children and I suffered. I now know I cannot ignore myself.' In that electric moment he was beside himself with happiness and lost no time arranging the marriage before she changed her mind.

She made a beautiful bride, dressed in a light pink lace dress, her carriage elegant. She looked happy in a quiet, subdued and understated way. To him the passage of years did not matter and had not erased or diminished anything. She confided in him, 'You were always alive somewhere in the recesses of my mind, though I could not call out to you. The cry was stifled within me before it could give itself a voice. It lay dormant, ready to kindle at the right time.'

It was not a fiery relationship for they were in the twilight of their years. It was quiet and still. There was never a passion to ignite, the solace in being together overwhelmed them into a contentment and happiness mode. There were not many people in their lives now, for most had outlived their heyday and were spent. They carried only their own weight, or the weight of each other, which was no burden at all. They incubated no fears except of losing each other. They were not daunted by each other's aging. They were soul mates.

The years kept sliding by faster than they could imagine. Then, with time a strange pallor emerged on her face and her emaciated body gave away telltale signs. Not able to hold himself back, he asked her gently, 'What ails you dearest?' She broke down crying, 'I am sick. It is terminal, I know it is!' He held her for a long time, until her sobbing subsided. All those years of waiting had not broken his spirit the way this did. All those years of endurance had broken hers, and finally her body set itself up to end it all. He knew he was the last breath she inhaled. She knew she was the last breath he inhaled. Then he made a pledge to himself that took him by surprise. This time he knew he had to do it for himself. He prepared himself to embrace the kiss of death. He felt only a tremor. She felt only a tremor. For too long they had been used to pain, having lived with its camaraderie. This time was no different.

CRUMBLY TIDBITS ON THE FLOOR

Mina lay sprawled on the floor, her long floral dress spread out in an ungainly fashion as she mindlessly munched cookies, helping herself from the packet that lay beside her. Her eyes wore a glazed look, her mind and body were attuned only to the act of chewing. Crumbly tidbits that scattered on the floor didn't seem to bother her at all. She was an obese woman with flabby arms from which layers of flesh hung loosely. She had a placid look, like that of a benign monster, with her puffed cheeks, thick lips and round flat nose with flaring nostrils.

'Mina! Mina! What are you doing lying here in the dark all alone? The house is in a mess and you lounge here, oblivious of everything,' called Zaif as he entered the room and saw his wife lying on the cluttered floor.

Mina stirred slowly, pouted and said sullenly, 'What's all the commotion about? Can't you ever leave me in peace?' Her outburst somewhat relieved her and she settled back as she had been.

'Don't you get tired of lounging around the whole day doing nothing?' snapped Zaif.

'Why do you resent my moments of leisure, after all I am not a maid in this house who works round the clock,' retorted Mina. 'I've raised five children and obviously I have not performed this onerous task merely by lounging around all day.'

'That is what you think! Get up and for heaven's sake do something useful!'

'Like what?' she said coldly.

'Like knit or sew or even paint as other women do.'

'I am not interested in petty things! I'd rather rest my nerves sleeping.'

'Then hibernate all your life. I have no patience for these things. I, for one, have decided to remain active until the end!'

'Well, that's your choice. Leave me alone with what is desirable to me.' Having said this she shut her eyes, conveying to him that the subject was closed.

By now Zaif's patience was drained and he stormed out of the house, banging the door. Usually a calm man, he had his limits.

Outside, the evening was still except for the distant hum of voices, the sounds of people returning home. As he looked at the windows of the neighbouring houses standing monolithic and silent, he wondered whether it was all a sham, this outward calm and quiet. He could not be the only one whose life was in turmoil. Mina was lost to him and he led a loveless existence.

The five children, all boys, were grown and now had an existence of their own. He had been very involved in caring for the boys when they were young as Mina had always been too self-involved and lazy to be able to keep up with the physical demands of looking after a large family.

Zaif had tried to be both a father and a mother to them, grooming them to be well-mannered boys, though they later developed behaviours bordering on delinquency. School had been tough for them and he was thankful there were no dropouts or expulsions, although there were plenty of complaints from their teachers about their mischief and bad behaviour. He polished his parenting skills - his military training had bolstered his stamina and helped him cope. He put his own needs aside while focusing on his sons. He felt he deserved a badge of honour for raising five boys who had been quite a handful. Now they were all married and settled in faraway cities, busy with their own lives.

Mina, for her part, had no feelings for him and treated him like a wayside stone, negligible in worth.

Trudging through the now deserted streets he reached the house of the woman who lately had become the focus of his thoughts. She was Laila, an artist of repute, residing a few kilometres away. She was an elegant woman with striking features, younger than he was. He had come to know that she was divorced and had children. That could be quite a handful, but he was accustomed to carrying loads. He had visited the art gallery where she was the curator and had conversed at length with her. He found her to be an outgoing, intelligent woman, knowledgeable about art. She told him that she had her own studio at her home. He was attracted by her passion for art and felt alive in her company.

He paused outside her house which was dark. He was tempted to knock on the door, but thought it improper. He would do this another day, he thought. Age had instilled caution in him, made him wary of certain situations.

Lights in nearby houses were being turned off as he turned to go back. He quietly entered his house, stepping stealthily into the bedroom and slipped between the cold sheets. He lay brooding until sleep overcame him.

The next day was Eid and Mina was cheerful and light-hearted, having dressed for the occasion. Sweetmeats and other delicacies were laid out on tables and she helped herself with relish. When a few guests dropped by to join in the celebrations she lay back in her armchair half dozing, smug and satiated. She was disinterested and lost in her world. Her guests took offence and left shortly. Zaif shook his head at her, his nerves testy. What a wife he had wasted his life on! Though he had become accustomed to her ways he did not consider himself ready to give up on life.

He ran into Laila frequently. He met her at art exhibitions, at the gallery and at friends' houses. Each time he felt born again, resuscitated from a kind of death. Laila had a way of filling the room with glowing warmth and good cheer. The sound of her voice was music to his ears, not boisterous, but pleasantly mellow. Her good humour lifted him out of his perpetual sadness. It seemed that finally doors were opening up for him. He knew he must do something quickly.

It was six months before he summoned the courage to tell Mina that he was leaving her for good. She responded in a measured tone, 'Go then, isn't it already too late? You have lost your youth, you are an old man.' He was stunned by her cold reply.

'I did it for *you*…you would have been devastated otherwise! You and the boys couldn't possibly have survived without me.' He was pushing his words out, throwing them out before remorse overcame him. He was a kind man and could not deal a cold blow. The truth was that he had never loved her yet she had given him five children whom he loved, and he was grateful for that. Though he had regretted his decision to marry her every day of his life, he had never thought of leaving her until now.

'You don't have to worry about me,' she continued coldly, but in a subdued voice. 'I can take care of myself.' He was stunned at her cool reaction for he had expected her to become hysterical, curse him and pour invectives on him. Yet she sat there, calmly giving her consent. It was as if she had been expecting this all these years, waiting for the moment when he would tell her he was leaving her. They both realised that this was inevitable, such was their fate. This was the first time since he had known her that he felt a sudden and unexpected rush of compassion.

That day Mina slipped away out of his life, leaving the city where she had merely existed to return to the city of her birth.

Soon after Zaif proposed to Laila, the woman he loved. For a man who had for so many years dwelt in cold indifference, he finally knew it was never too late to follow one's heart.

Settling back at her mother's home, Mina spread herself on the couch, opened her bag of cookies and started to munch slowly, her entire attention focused on her favourite television series. It was a seemingly ordinary day. Her mother stood in the shadows, looking at her daughter wistfully, a look that was as hopeless as it was melancholy.

GONE WITH THE WINTER WINDS

'Madam, I am sorry to say it's all over. The cancer has metastasized all through his body,' the doctor said grimly. 'We tried everything, nothing worked. The cancer has devoured him.'

Sheherazade stared at the doctor with glazed uncomprehending eyes. Surely she had not heard right? This man standing before her in a white coat was saying things which her mind could not register. Her head was spinning.

She looked at his face and wanted to shout 'Stop!' But no, she must restrain herself and not break down in front of him. He continued in a sympathetic tone, 'Your husband is dying; he has just a few more days. I'm sorry I can't do anything. Only a miracle can save him now.' He shook his head helplessly.

'But doctor you had said that you would try a new experimental drug. You gave us hope and now you say it is all finished - all finished, just like that!' she burst out. 'My beloved husband's precious life is just shutting down like a battery.'

'I'm sorry for him and for your family. But I must say I admire his tenacity for he is a great fighter. There was never an iota of self-pity in him, only a steely determination to combat the disease.' After a pause he continued softly, 'He values his life the same way he would value another's. He is so much together all the time, holding himself with dignity, more concerned about you and the family than of himself. He followed in detail my advice and the treatment we administered to him. Your husband is a real gentleman in every sense of the word. God does not make such men every day.' Was she mistaken or did she see his eyes become misty! Her heart softened towards him.

Sheherazade walked out of the hospital feeling drained and numb, her mind failing to register the finality of the hours. How could Jehangir's life be snuffed out like a candle in such a short time? He was too precious to her and to so many others, and such people can't just evaporate from this world, like smoke from a fire. She put her chin up in denial, pondering how a solid mountain like him could possibly be swept away by the first winds of winter.

How would she face him now, look into his eyes, and tell him that his life was slipping away and out of his control! How could it all end, their dreams to build their lives together and those of their children?

When she entered the house, he was reclining in their living room waiting for her. He was a tall man, but lately seemed to have shrunk, his body frame hunched. Still despite his frailty, he did not look like a man whose life was fast ebbing away. How deceptive life could be shrouding the spectre of death inside. As she nervously sat beside him, he pulled her towards him and she clung to him, silently begging him not to leave her. She wanted to tell him that he was all she had, had ever had. Her life had revolved around him for so long that she did not know how she would move on. But her lips would not move, lest she betray herself.

'What did the doctor say, darling?' he asked her gently, his eyes on her, his voice faltering like a reed in the wind.

She sucked in her breath before she could speak, ‘He repeated they would try a new experimental drug on you. He hopes it will make a difference.’

He smiled weakly, ‘Yes, if God be willing. But you must not worry darling, it never pays to worry. We will cross the bridges when we come to them.’ She could not hold back the tears which he appeared not to notice. He continued, ‘I love you! Our love is like a burning coal that knows no boundaries of time and space.’ What does he mean? Does he know time is running out? She was wracked by anxiety.

The servant brought in the tea tray and they sat pensively, sipping the strongly brewed tea. For once he was not communicative but lost in thought. She longed to say something, but then silence was a kind of refuge. It allowed her mind to drift into faraway territory, a much-needed escape for her. She turned away from his drawn, tightly stretched face, it was too painful to watch. The cancer was taking its toll.

All through their years together they had mindfully nurtured their relationship. She had been young and immature when they married. She was a shy reticent girl, having led a protected life under her parents' umbrella. Jehangir was the opposite - outgoing, garrulous and forever surrounded by friends. He pulled her gently out of her shell and bolstered her confidence. He told her how much he loved her looks, her style and the way she talked and carried herself. He said, ‘We must create strong bonds between us that stand steadfast in the test of time. You must check me whenever I am at fault - I am a very fallible person.'

He had a close and loving relationship with their three daughters, Sara, Sana and Sasha, and spent a lot of time with them despite a busy schedule. Yet when it came to discipline, he was a stickler. When his daughter, Sara, was going abroad to study he admonished her, 'No alcohol and no boys, both will lead you astray from work.'

'Oh, Papa, you and your fears! You know me well!' she had laughed, but he was serious. He knew the hazards that lay for young people studying abroad. He was happy that she remained true to her word. Later, when she came of age and was ready for marriage, he warned her again, 'Remember you must marry a Muslim boy, the sect or creed is not a matter of concern to me. We must minimise the cultural differences.' Such was his vision of life.

He was the head of a manufacturing firm that he had started from scratch, establishing and building it with diligence and perseverance. He managed his business with a strict hand and did not tolerate disobedience of his code of ethics. He did not hesitate to lay off anyone who went against his principles. Those who put in hard work were rewarded well and given support to grow professionally. He attended to their needs as if they were his children. His employees would proudly say, 'He is my mentor who will see me grow and become strong. I owe everything to him.' For them he was compassionate and mindful, helping them shape their careers. They knew they could rely on him as long as they remained true to his value system. He knew how to mould the lives of young employees with understanding and empathy.

Jehangir's business flourished with a dedicated team of young, qualified and committed men and women who worked diligently to make the company a success. He knew his employees were his valuable asset and he rewarded them with financial compensations and awards. On one occasion, at an award ceremony, he was overcome with emotion whilst paying them tribute. His voice trembled as he said, 'This company owes each of you a debt. This success would not have been possible without your struggle.' He was a sensitive and tolerant man and could feel the pulse of his workers - a rare quality.

Sheherazade and Jehangir enjoyed a rich and fulfilled life together. They entertained extravagantly and invited people from all spheres of life. Jehangir was well-connected as having alliances served several practical purposes. Sheherazade went along with him in every activity. They were partners and best friends. He told her, 'We must work on our relationship, tell me when I act like an ogre and I will tell you when you act like one. The beauty of our lives is the ability to change. This is the ultimate triumph and our ultimate goal,' He was no ideologue, but had the humility to see inwards, to recognise his faults and to mend them.

Jehangir had a close relationship with his mother who was a graceful, polished woman. They shared many things together and had a common world-view. He would sometimes complain that she treated him like a child instead of a grown man, to which she would reply, 'A child is always a child for his mother! To this day I see in you a defiant little boy, with a mind of his own and with a heart of gold.'

'Mother your little boy has come a long way, though still struggling, for that never ceases. Never stop praying for me. I am not self-complacent, yet I believe I have achieved measurable wholeness with age. You and Pa taught me never to give up on myself. I lost him a long time ago, but his integrity and dignity still resonate in me.' Mother and son sadly clung to the memory of the dead man who had left them years ago.

Now as Sheherazade watched him from the corner of her eyes, she saw a man torn apart with disease. The cancer treatment had taken up most of his last three precious years, but he was a born fighter and lived life fully and completely, even in such a situation. During this period, they had gone on holidays together knowing that these opportunities might not come again. He had been vivacious and joyful, more than usual, as he made the most of every moment. Ironically, he had learnt that he valued life more in adversity than when the going was good.

Now his three daughters - ever present, ever vigilant - sat across from him. They knew time was running out. He beckoned to them gently with a wave of his hand, and kissed them. 'Remember darlings, I shall always love you from the depths of my heart. You taught me to love completely and to forget myself in loving you. Your mother,' he looked at his wife, 'taught me the many manifestations of love - tolerance, patience and unconditional love. I was a barren man before I met her.'

As night fell the family fell asleep in one room, afraid to leave him for even a moment. Darkness gathered outside, folding itself into a grey mantle. Through the window a whimsical moon was gliding between clouds that played hide and seek. Finally sleep overtook the beleaguered family.

Suddenly Sheherazade awoke in a state of panic. The room was icy cold. There was the stillness of death in the room. She glanced at Jehangir lying beside her. He was not breathing, his body motionless. She touched his hand, it was cold. She smothered a cry. The dim light creeping into the room lit his face. He had a serene, placid expression and the pain from his face was erased by the hand of death. The end had come and death had stolen the most precious being in her life.

Outside the world was buzzing with people starting their day's activity, but for her the silence inside was louder than anything she had ever known. She was conscious of fatigue creeping through her body like poison. All these past months she had not felt like this as hope had resonated. And now a great fear overwhelmed her as she looked at her sleeping daughters. She must waken them and break the terrible news! She said a silent prayer, asking God to give her the strength to carry her through that dreadful day.

JENNIFER

There was a performance in the city that day to which people flocked in droves. The star performer was an English poet, Jennifer, a tall, robust woman. In the large hall packed with an eager audience, her voice resonated with her songs sung in a lilting voice. English poetry was, as a norm, read and seldom sung, but she aligned herself with the tone and rhythm of the music in her adopted land, where poetry in Urdu was sung to the accompaniment of music. Jennifer breathed poetry in her daily life. It was the lifeblood circulating in her veins. It struck deep at a nerve, unseen, painful and intense, and she shuddered when it surfaced from within. It reflected the pathos of loss, loved ones torn apart, lost homeland and cryptic alienation. That was long ago, but it had settled itself deep in her mind, where daily spectres stalked from the past. Otherwise she had a strong sense of loyalty to her family.

The performance ended with fervent applause resonating across the hall. Jennifer was seen walking out holding hands with her brown-skinned husband, whom she loved ferociously.

Theirs was a mutual love that had its genesis in rebellion. She had fought long and hard battles with her English parents to wed this alien man from a different culture. They were terrified for their young daughter who aspired high, seeking the sky. Surprisingly, her husband had won acceptance from his family, though they knew they had lost him to his English wife. Nobody was sure it would last, but the couple surprised everyone. They were bound together in solidarity, mindful of each other's needs.

The passage of years did not diminish or fray their love. The many friends who straddled their lives saw gaps in their lives, she with her typical English ways, and he with his radical, *desi* mannerisms. He embarrassed her oftentimes with his outspoken ways, for he was a man given to candour. Jennifer embraced all of him, took it all in, and never demurred. They were closely bonded and in sync. They entertained guests lavishly at home, embraced each other's culture and became role models for their children.

Jennifer bore four children, two girls and two boys, who resembled their mother in her vitality and her flair for words. They had her auburn hair, fair complexions and light-coloured eyes. They loved their parents intensely and were fiercely loyal to them in spirit and deed. From their father they got a love of the land, for its *desi* food and for Urdu poetry. They were a united family with strong bonds.

And then their daughter, the youngest, fell sick with pneumonia, and Jennifer nursed her all day and all night. This six-year old child had curly, golden locks and adored her parents. She tossed feverishly with a rasping cough that didn't seem to abate. She became weaker and frailer, and her health rapidly deteriorated until one cold December morning she didn't wake up from her sleep. They buried her in their family graveyard so they could always be near her.

Jennifer and her husband were grief-stricken and mourned her death for years. In the process of grieving they lost each other and fell apart. Jennifer gave in to her distress, her husband looked distant and lost. He could not bear to see his grieving wife and her forlorn look, and after turning the crisis over in his mind, decided to leave the house. He believed this was the only way he could put a salve on his aching heart.

He didn't think for a moment that he was abandoning his wife and children, reassuring himself that he needed an escape from his grieving wife who had been central to his life. She had always been by his side - the time when he lost his job, even the time when he lost his fortune, foolishly squandering it away. She had not reproached him then, neither had she lost faith in him, and above all she had continued smiling.

Jennifer and the children were utterly broken when he went missing. They waited but there was no word from him. Finally, they lost hope and the children continued with their lives. Now Jennifer grieved for two people, her dead daughter and her husband. Somewhere in her mind she never lost hope.

She delved into poetry more than ever before, only now her verses were sombre and melancholy. Her frequent performances drew large audiences. She never told anyone her story, it was beyond telling, and she wore her grief like a shroud. She grew manic, attending every literary event in town, every musical evening and every reading, and immersed herself in her grief. She constantly craved applause and recognition. Her concerts were frequent and lucrative and she relished the attention. She became egotistical, throwing tantrums when she felt ignored. She grumbled, 'How can I not be invited - an important personality like me? I am the Nightingale of the East and no event is complete without me!' With such outbursts, doors were closing that never opened again.

She ruffled many feathers with her eccentric behaviour and gradually she felt herself alone and friendless. Her fans observed her change and wondered why this lyrical poet, who had the capacity to fly them to another fantasy place, was always on edge. They didn't know the woman's world had collapsed with her husband gone, her moorings were lost and poetry was her only catharsis.

During this time she courted a man and had an affair to muffle the terrible disquiet within her. The man took her seriously, flattered by her attention. When he tried to come closer, she pushed him away in revulsion, shunning him. She had only one love in her life, and that was her husband whom she yearned for daily. One day, in sheer desperation, he shamed her and called her a whore. She ended the affair. He made several attempts to see her again and each time was scorned by her. She was a lioness in her rage.

Years went by and Jennifer continued to wait for her husband. She also continued to light the candle of love in her heart.

Then one day he returned, like a long-lost lover. He looked haggard and was limping - a wretched piece of skin and bones. She saw him walking up the pathway of the house and was stunned. For a moment she froze, totally befuddled, betraying no emotion. He came up to her with his eyes averted and embraced her. He held her tightly for what seemed an eternity. Finally, she asked, 'Where have you been all these years? My God, you have changed.' He did not answer, the words rising to his mouth choked him with guilt. She took him inside, knowing something had died within him. That was why he had returned, not because he was resuscitated but because the last embers in him were burning out. It was an amalgam of loneliness and aging. He murmured vaguely, 'Am I back home? Will you take me in?' His words struck a dagger in Jennifer's heart and in that moment, she forgave him and his great betrayal. She had craved for normalcy in her life again and this time she could not let him go.

JOSHUA

The year was 1945. The war with Germany had ended and the Germans had been defeated by the Allies. The concentration camp at Auschwitz was closing down along with many others, where thousands of Jews had been incarcerated. We had survived brutal torture and mercifully we were still alive.

My Ma and I were put on board a ship where we were jammed together like sardines. As I looked around me I saw hundreds of my clan huddled together, all Jewish people. Our faces showed it all. Nobody had to ask and none of us needed to explain. We had everything in common, like caged animals. Our bodies were thin as scarecrows, our eyes hollow and there were little traces of emotion in them. Even animals show emotion, harangue, scream. But we did nothing of the sort. Most of us had forgotten our own names and remembered only the numbers by which we were identified. Our existence was nameless and faceless. Daily we had faced extinction in the camps, daily we died a death more grotesque than death itself. We were survivors, fighting and succumbing in one breath. We learnt how humans could survive by sheer force of will, dogged spirit and tenacity.

When we finally landed on the shores of America I felt, after many years, a tingling sensation of my body coming alive, of being reborn. I looked around and saw my Ma huddled beside me, a shrunken, wizened shadow of a once robust woman.

Pa was no longer with us, he had been arrested and taken away before us. We never heard from Pa again, but we knew his fate. A year later the Nazis came and took Ma and me to Auschwitz.

My adopted land was a sanctuary for Ma and me. It opened my life to a new panorama. I blended into a sea of nameless people. I felt myself healed by mixing with strangers and building bonds of friendship. I never looked back, though at times I found myself turning over my shoulder fearfully, to hear the crunch of military boots behind me, and when I turned there would be no one. My new milieu gave me a new life and opened new spaces both inside and outside of me.

New York was a bustling city of mixed races, easy to blend in, because of its ethnic diversity. I connected with members of my Jewish community, sharing their joys and tribulations. We were struggling youths, having much to contribute to each other in the form of physical support and a sense of togetherness. This bond with the other boys - David, Abel and Don - lasted a lifetime. We were brothers in our common turmoil of displacement. We poured our hearts out to each other in a world that was strange, but that was growing on us. We struggled for a foothold in this new world, to become acclimatised to its culture and norms. The American dream was coming alive as we struggled to build from the ashes of our former lives.

I blended in with the white Americans but I was different as well, with my sharp, angular features. New York suited me as I grew taller and stronger. Ma would call me her handsome young man! She would, however, also admonish me to stand straight and not hunch my back in an apologetic posture. I told her that I did not like her remarks. I am proud of my heritage, of belonging to a brave community. She sighed, 'Joshua, my son, you will never understand!'

When I would retort, 'I am not a fool, Ma!'

She would reply, 'Son, you take offence too easily. I suppose it's your youth.' I wished Ma would not caution me all the time. It instils a spectre of fear in me.

As we settled into our new life, I wanted Ma to put the past behind her and move on, but she continued to brood. 'Don't forget the past, we learn from it.' She was superstitious, afraid my success would attract the evil eye. I reassured her, telling her to be happy for us. We had travelled far and uphill, and now people looked up to us in awe, begging for favours.

Ma was a strong believer in God, she prayed and thanked the Almighty Lord for his magnanimity. She baked cakes and cookies to distribute to neighbours to keep the evil eye away. 'We are blessed when we serve God's humanity. Good neighbourliness dissolves social barriers.' Her wisdom has stayed with me through time.

However, Ma was lonely, overcome by bouts of anxiety often triggered by a small incident. One day when I returned from work I found her crying at the kitchen table. 'Oh Joshua, the women in the neighbourhood keep their distance from me. They are culturally far apart. Our neighbour is not concerned that her daughter lives with her boyfriend out of wedlock. Now isn't that outrageous, Joshua? When I express my views, they look at me scornfully, as if I am from another world. Joshua, do you think we are that different?' she asked wide-eyed. Speechless, I embraced her tightly, unable to console her, as her tears flowed uncontrollably.

After this incident I decided to move to another neighbourhood which was a predominantly Jewish locality. It was a picturesque area, thronged with markets and a synagogue where Ma could go for prayer. I prayed she would adapt better with her own kind. And she did! I was delighted at the change in her. She was light-hearted and socialised with women her age and had found her comfort zone. When I would come back from work, she would narrate stories to me about visits to neighbours, 'You know Joshua, our neighbour Eva comes from Poland. She lived close to where we lived. She and her husband left Poland before the war started and were spared our agony. They have been living here since. She has two children, a son and daughter, both married, and three grandchildren whom she adores. She has invited us to dinner tomorrow.'

I was amazed. 'Ma, your endearing ways earned you a quick invitation.' She squeezed my hand delightedly.

The next day Ma dressed in a pretty grey dress that she had not used for years. It was a long time since she had dressed so carefully. She styled a new hairdo and her curly locks softened her sharp features. She was finally coming into her own.

The dinner went well, with animated conversation and delicious home-cooked food served on hot platters. Eva and her husband Jericho were an amiable couple. Jericho was stout, jovial and quick-witted in contrast to his quiet wife. He joked with her affectionately, 'My wife is an excellent cook, but I know at the end of the day she'll kill me with her tempting desserts. "Good riddance to you!" she will say!'

'You are blessed, dear man, to have her keep your house in such an impeccable condition,' Ma spoke up loyally for her friend.

'Madam, I am only a lodger in this house, my wife is the commandant!'

They laughed, enjoying his jokes, whilst Eva looked on warmly. She was used to her husband's humour.

When the conversation turned to our common birthplace, Poland, a cold sombre air drifted in. The memories were fraught with pain. We realised the agony of displacement stays for a lifetime. Such deep scars never heal.

Eva whispered in a low voice. 'We knew earlier the future would hold suffering or death and were desperate to leave. The Nazis were gradually closing in. In this atmosphere of fear and anxiety we planned to escape before it was too late.'

As I looked at Ma, I was afraid she might break down, as fearful spectres from the past emerged in her mind again. I got up to call it a day. We effusively thanked our hosts and left. On our way home, my mother took my arm, 'You know Joshua, memories of the past have returned today. Eva and Jericho did not witness what we did, and do not carry our painful baggage. They can laugh and be happy in this foreign land.' She sighed heavily, her grip tightening on my arm until I winced. I watched her with an aching heart.

I can never forget the day I brought Haifa, a Palestinian employee in my office, to my home. She was amiable and soft-spoken, but could be assertive when necessary. Ma was furious - I didn't expect such a reaction from her! She eyed her from head to foot with her sharp, eagle-eyed look and said, 'Joshua tells me you are from Palestine.'

The girl, sensing Ma's hostility, nervously replied, 'My parents migrated to the US five years back. Our country is eternally a war-zone and the future was bleak for us children, with more than half the youth unemployed. This forced my parents to take this great step.'

Ma continued in the same tone, 'My dear, you ought to know the land of our birth is our eternal stamp. There is no escaping it. And how come you are a friend of my son, girl?' she added sternly.

I knew I had to interpose, 'Ma, she works in my office.'

I was relieved, Ma was nonplussed and spoke not another word.

When Haifa left, Ma turned on me, 'Joshua, have you gone crazy, bringing a Palestinian girl into my house? Aren't you familiar with our situation?'

'Why Ma, you are a prisoner of your fears. We have our differences, but they are political. Haifa is sympathetic, we share a similar pain of being dispossessed. She claims Jewish people are closer to Palestinians in the way they practice their rituals. I pray at some point the two will put their differences aside and reconcile.'

'Joshua you were only a young boy when we came here. You remember the Nazis, how they dragged us out of our homes, raped, tortured and killed us. What we went through was horrific and my wounds are still festering. And now the Arabs are after our blood, they want the Israelis out of the land, our old Jewish heritage. Where should this race go then? Joshua, promise me to be always on your guard.'

How could I tell Ma that she was punishing her own self? She had to let go, as we do of a loved one who is gone. We don't have a choice. I consider myself lucky. I have youth on my side. The world opens to me when I embrace it. I do not hold back. I grasp every opportunity and explore new avenues for myself. My journey is a long one and I have a long way to go.

I looked sadly at Ma. What did she have? She lacked the strength to walk this huge vibrant city. It did not take to her - she won't breathe its fresh air, won't open the windows of her mind. Her solace is her memories. The man she loved is gone. The old world she grew up in is gone. She does not take to the new order. It does not take to her; then where should she go? The ghosts of the past lurk in her inner closet.

One day I found Ma crying as she watched the pouring rain. 'You know, Joshua, it was such a day when heavens were pouring tears from stormy eyes, that they came to take your Pa away. I ran after them, begged them not to take him from me. The Nazi officer struck me with his gun and I fell down the steps. My forehead was bleeding, but the Nazi officer spat on the ground and walked away. I still have the scar from that day. Look Joshua, here!' She pulled her white hair away from her forehead to reveal a deep scar. 'Joshua, if humans do not have compassion for each other, they do not deserve to be called human.'

I alone understood her in this whole world. I was all she had now. That is why she held on to me like a drowning person. I know she will not welcome another woman in my life, even if that woman is my wife. She cannot share me with anybody and will unknowingly make my life miserable. There is a price for everything in life.

....

Years later, when I went to visit Ma in the institution where she now lived, she barely recognised me. I was saddened to see her fading slowly into a murky world of her own. It was ironic, the past she had clung to was lost in the desolate landscape of her mind. She kissed and hugged me as she quietly took the flowers I had brought for her, looking at me with smudged eyes as she inhaled their fragrance. She sighed, 'Your father always brought me these flowers.' Then there was silence between us, not a cold silence, but that of two people who find solace in each other's presence. Words now carried no meaning as the curtain was ready to fall. I felt an aching pain.

When she saw me rise, her eyes pleaded with mine to stay. I glimpsed a flicker of recognition, the haunted look of an animal, lost in its rootlessness. 'Are you leaving?' Then looking at the graying darkness outside, she said, 'Yes, you must leave now. It is getting dark. Go carefully, son, the road is ridden with thieves.' I quickly took my leave and left without looking back.

I was agonised by her situation, but helpless, for she was destined for this life, and I was for mine. I had married Haifa, and now my blood and hers runs in the veins of our children. She was the gentle bird destined to fly into my window and build a nest in its tangled branches. I know Ma would never have approved, but I had to do this for myself and for her as well. After all, Ma always taught me to be human. And Ma wanted her bloodline to continue after she passed on.

LIFE IS ALL ABOUT GRIT

The girl's face was marked with deep scars, having been afflicted with chickenpox in childhood. These marred an otherwise pretty face with well-defined features. Her mother cringed when anyone alluded to her daughter's scars, 'Can you not treat them in any way? You know she is a girl,' they would delicately chide her. The mother would reply simply, 'The infection spread quickly, the attack was severe and the marks are permanent.'

When the girl came of age she was married to a good-looking but sickly man. People passed snide remarks, 'She has got what she deserved.' They didn't realise the depth of their cruelty. The boy she married was easy-going and they enjoyed an amicable relationship with minimal conflict. He was not put off by her scars and was in the habit of tenderly stroking them with his long thin fingers. He told her they were part of her unique signature style. Nothing ever ruffled him and he healed her in many ways with his accepting manner.

They had two children, a girl and a boy who were the joy of their lives. The couple's life was complete, their marital life was bliss. He worked as a clerk in a local office and whatever money he made was enough for them. Their needs were small and she, not having been spoilt in her childhood, was content with what she had.

Then tragedy struck and he suffered a bout of pneumonia. He had been born with a congenital condition that had affected his weak lungs and this made his condition serious and unstable. The girl was distraught and nursed him round the clock, but his condition deteriorated and finally he died. She was heartbroken and her two offspring were now her only support in an otherwise empty life. The children bore resemblance to their father and both reminded her of him.

The woman had in her life drawn her boundaries with precision. She expected little from people and got little in return. She was a virtuous woman whose intentions were always good and she had no reason to think others could doubt her intentions. She did not know that people had malicious intent and a habit of weaving stories from overly imaginative minds that were otherwise void and dull.

After her husband's death she had the liberty to make her own choices. She struggled with a small job to make ends meet for her two children, which wasn't easy but not impossible. The children managed to get into college, and after graduation the son was employed as a clerk in a large state-owned company and moved to another town. The girl also graduated and got a job as a teacher in a private school and also moved to another town. The widow was left alone again, but she was content that her children were happy and settled. Then one day when she was at work, busy stitching garments, her boss, who had been making overtures at her for some time, physically assaulted her. He told her flatly, 'If you value this job, you will have to do what I tell you!' She quit the same day.

Then a friend offered her a job at her husband's store. She considered herself lucky and accepted the offer. Now she was financially independent and did not need to borrow from anyone. Meanwhile her neighbours, not content to sit idle, watched the woman live by herself without male support. They could not fathom that. 'Look at her guts, living alone, supporting herself. What is her source of income?' Word circulated that her income was illicit and ill-gotten. Neighbours began to ostracise her and the woman's isolation increased. Endurance had taught her many lessons and patiently she put up with their whispers.

A few years later she married her daughter to a young man whom she selected from her kin. He was a practical, hard-working man, with enough grit to make things work. The daughter, a sober young girl, did not leave her job and did not move in with her husband. The husband continued to work in a town away from her. This arrangement was agreeable to both and did not diminish their love in any way.

But the women in the widow's town were upset by this unusual arrangement and voiced their disapproval 'They will regret this one day!' Their anger was fueled when she turned a deaf ear to their vicious remarks. They dished out dirt about her daughter as well, alleging that she was up to no good having the audacity to live away from her husband. 'Today's girls are shamelessly independent, as if their husbands don't matter anymore. She's a pretty girl and must flaunt her beauty to lure other men. There must be some other reason why she lives alone.' The widow ignored the neighbours and continued to trust her daughter enough and did not interfere.

Then her son-in-law got a job in the widow's city. The woman decided to offer her son-in-law a room in her house, to make matters easy for him. The son-in-law accepted and moved in, hoping to save some money in this way. The daughter thanked her mother for her kindness. The neighbours were shocked by this arrangement. Very soon they began to gossip again and spun bizarre stories. Word circulated that the widow was having an affair with her son-in-law. One lady alleged, 'I saw them through my window, sitting close together. I say they are up to no good! We must act immediately!' Collectively the neighbours stoked a fire and forced them to evacuate the house. The widow and son-in-law moved to another locality far away from her vicious neighbours where nobody knew them.

Eventually the widow acknowledged her grave error. Her good intentions had become fodder for the rumour mill. It was too late to undo the mistakes of the past, but it so happened that through her unfailing grit, she stood tall and unbroken. She had stood like a bulwark behind her children when they were little, and they were unharmed by the storms that brewed around them. When they grew up, they did well for themselves. The son married a well-to-do, educated girl, rose to become the mayor in the town, and the daughter and her husband both earned handsome salaries. Their lives changed when the entire family moved to a posh locality, where they were very popular and respected. The widow now understood the bounties that she had been blessed with and lived a fulfilled life.

LIVING ON THE EDGE

Sophia sat on the patio, composed and serene, surrounded by lush, freshly watered plants. She was much advanced in years, but her silver plaited hair was camouflaged with brown hair dye. One could tell at a glance that she had been beautiful in her prime. Spirited in her younger days, she had morphed into a subdued person and wore a resigned look. Her eyes were glazed with a peculiar hollowness in them. It was as if somebody had put out their light. Colourfully dressed like a mannequin in a shop window, she was elegant, but mute and hollow. Her gnarled hands clumsily knitted balls of wool into a scarf. She had to keep herself busy or inertia would be her death.

She was alerted to the sound of footsteps to her left. It was her daughter who had just come on to the patio. Her beautiful daughter in the prime of her life moved in another hemisphere, vibrant with energy and life. When she talked, it was from another world. 'Mother, it's too cold for you to sit here. The sun has set and taken away its warmth with it. You'll catch a chill.' The old lady shook her head and said slowly, '*Meri jaan*, the sun has taken away its heat, but what about the warmth inside me? It still glows like an eternal light. That's what really matters.' Her daughter laughed and retorted, still from another plane, 'Now, Mother, here you go philosophical again, not thinking of your frailty. Nobody can beat you!' Sophia sighed for she knew her daughter could not understand because she had never walked in her shoes. '*Meri jaan!* Carry on with what you were doing and leave me to my own devices. Can't you see I don't have the energy to stir my old creaky bones? Leave me to my memories, they are all I have now, my everlasting gems.'

She heaved a sigh of relief as her daughter left, leaving the patio door slightly ajar. She loved her, but the girl rankled her peace when all she wanted was to be alone. Her thoughts flashed through a labyrinth of years that was her life's journey. She had been a pretty young woman pulsing with energy and had married the man with whom she had fallen in love. It was love at first sight. She had looked into the mirror of his eyes and seen herself, so transparent was he. It was mostly smooth sailing except for her tempestuous outbursts that erupted on occasion. She would bemoan his meagre wallet and his insensitivity to her needs, but he would fold her into his arms and hold her long until her body was still, 'There, now my baby, it's all over. I promise I will take a loan from my employer and buy you that pretty necklace you saw in that store on Fleming Street.' The air between them would clear quickly afterwards. He forgave easily and there was never any rancour.

Tears slid down her cheeks as she recalled those moments. He had pampered her, knowing she had always got what she wanted, having been raised by indulgent parents. He had married above his station and he paid the price. But she was his prize and this made his generous heart swell with pride. There had been a constant trickle of gold trinkets and pretty silk dresses which he lavished on her. He would have fallen into debt if it had gone on for much longer.

He had a sudden heart attack and was gone in minutes before assistance came. He died cradled in her arms like a child. For many years after her life stood still and she wept and grieved to her heart's content so that her loss would not fester inside her. But the years of widowhood were long, solitary and daunting, where like a lone warrior she had braced the highs and lows. Men patronised her, looked upon her as weak and in need of support. A few proposed marriage to her, attracted by her alluring beauty and her zest for life. She had refused them all because in her heart she still loved the man of her dreams. Women shook their heads with pity at her lonely situation, not that they offered any help. But she knew her strength and was guided by her own solitary light.

That was a long time ago and much water had passed under the bridge, making her seasoned and worldly wise. Her parents before her had weathered many storms and had been hardened by them. Her sorrows too had toughened her body's slender contours and life flowed back with vigour. Her daughters helped to revive her spirits and she became alive, albeit a part of her bore the scar. She stood like a backbone for them so that they would not fall apart. Her eyes lit up at the sight of them, two butterflies fluttering in the wind, unprepared for the ensuing storms. She gave them unconditional love so they could weather any turbulence. And now they were returning it to her in full measure by their concern for her. She had carefully chosen their life partners for them, those whose coffers were full so they would never have to face hard times.

Her largess overflowed and embraced her siblings, ten in all, and she shared years of merriment and joy with them. They were fiery birds of one feather, one genetic code, rollicking with mirth, generous to a fault. They steeped themselves in life's gaiety, denying themselves nothing. They lived in luxury and ate well. They talked volubly, lighting up social gatherings by being the centre of any party. They loved excessively and fought rowdily. They were intoxicated in their love for the Divine and their surrender to Him was absolute. They did not dwell on anything too long or too deeply, being naturally restless by temperament. Then one by one they departed for their eternal abode and Sophia was the only sibling left to mourn their loss.

There was no one to share her loneliness. Her hands trembled at the thought. Her eye fell on her lean hands, veins snaking intricately, and she rubbed them vigorously to ease the stiffness. How the years had flown since her beloved man had held her soft hands and kissed them gently. She still loved him dearly, more than ever before. Her love was absolute even after his death.

One day her beloved daughter, Marium, broke the news, 'Mother I have been diagnosed with cancer and the doctor has said that it is in the third stage.' With that mother and daughter broke down and wept. Sophia wailed, 'It's my time to go, not yours. You will recover my darling. Life cannot swing backwards.' Her daughter was consoled and her wild eyes softened.

Then started the excruciating treatments in which her lovely daughter grew emaciated and pale. Soon she was too weak to continue with the treatments and needed to be hospitalised. Inevitably, the call came one night and Sophia rushed to the hospital. She was in time to hold her daughter's hand before death claimed her. Marium wept and clung to her mother, her eyes filled with fear. 'Please don't let me go Mother. I'm not yet ready.' Then she tossed and turned and gasping for breath, breathed her last. Something inside Sophia broke forever the day Marium was buried - a part of her was severed from her, it was like losing a limb. She was left to wonder, 'Does my Creator really think I am strong enough to bear all this?' This time she had not wailed, but stood tall and contained her great grief. She did not want to let go of her grief, it was her old-age ally in solitude.

Sophia put aside her knitting needles and rose from her chair to move her stiff limbs, but felt dizzy and fell back into the chair. 'Age is catching up in more ways than one.' The rolls of scarves she had knitted fell to her feet and bending painfully she collected them in her arms.

One day shortly after this she collapsed and was rushed to hospital. There she lay gasping for breath and just when hope was gone, she opened her eyes and looked smilingly at her family hovering around her bed. 'My darlings! Did you really think I would leave you so soon? It would take a very strong push to run me down.' They hugged and kissed her one by one. She was a fighter and was not ready to surrender yet. She had been given a new lease on life.

With every passing year an increasing weakness was taking over her body. Her thoughts riddled her. Most of her contemporaries were no more, she had lost too much. How many more deaths would she see before the final knell! Did her daughter who stood gently shaking her and affectionately scolding her, 'Wake up, Mother,' not know that she was living with the phantoms of the past and the spectre of mortality. How could a withering flower, discoloured and brittle, be revived? A breath of spring could not and would not inject new life into it. A sigh escaped her lips.

Inside her mind the haunting silence grew louder and deafening. She was anesthetised, empty. Her vacant eyes were shut and her body slumped. In the midst of this silence a cry was heard from inside the house, it was her daughter who let out a heart-wrenching scream. Sophia knew the long wait was over and the final challenge, last but not least, had to be crossed with composure. She had always told her daughter, 'The tide flows in one direction, if it turns around, it leaves a deeply scarred ridge.' She had lived with that scar for too long and knew it was time to let go.

LOVE AT FIRST SIGHT

Lyla was convinced she was in love with the boy. He was handsome and amiable and had a self-assured swagger that she found irresistible. Lyla was no less a catch, being poised, educated and belonging to an upper middle-class family with a good standing in society. The boy's family had acquired new wealth by climbing the ladder of success with quick fixes and short-cuts.

Lyla and the boy dated secretly in defiance of the boy's conservative family who did not approve of this. Lyla's family was more liberal and less rigid in their world-view and she enjoyed some relative freedom.

The boy was completely enamoured of Lyla. He fawned on her, adulated her and worked hard at winning her attention. She had never felt this way before - being placed on a pedestal like a princess and made to feel so special. He would say effusively, 'You are the prettiest girl in the world, I have never met anyone with such charm, grace and intelligence.' Lyla was ecstatic, she had never heard such amorous words gushing out from a suitor before. She had been lavished abundant love and attention by her parents as she was their only child. But for Lyla this time was different. When she lay in his arms, he coddled her like a baby, saying, 'You are the love of my life, the reason for my being.' And as he held her, he could feel her body tremble. She listened to every word he uttered, believing in him, yet knowing him not at all.

Lyla was raised in a special way, nurtured and delicately groomed by her parents, and as she grew older, she burgeoned into an attractive young girl with curly brown hair and pink, high cheekbones. Her parents did not expose her to the ugly realities of life and theirs was a life of luxury and comfort and empty of conflict in any form. They gave her a liberal education in elite institutions. When her savvy suitor, who inhabited the real world of wily politics and trade, proposed to her, she gave her consent with a spontaneity and quickness that surprised even him. She had proved an easy catch!

When Lyla informed her mother, she was shocked, 'Oh my God! What have you done? You barely know him! My sweet innocent child, I'm terrified of this action of yours. I fervently pray you don't live to regret it!' Lyla threw a tantrum, stamped her feet and screamed, and the mother was silenced. The mother knew and feared the naivete of youth, and she shuddered.

After that Lyla shut herself in her room for days and would not speak or eat. The distraught parents began to see the writing on the wall - they were heartbroken but decided to go along with their daughter's wishes. They didn't want to lose their precious daughter in the process. The anguished father was also torn between love and discipline, understanding the pitfalls of both. However, both parents curbed their fears and gave their consent, praying all would go well.

When the boy announced to his parents that he was marrying a girl in the neighbourhood they were outraged at the idea of their son getting married to a virtual stranger. The father confronted the son, shouted and cursed at him, 'Are you mad, taking this decision on your own. Such girls who marry without their parent's involvement are bold and not trustworthy! Tomorrow she can leave you for somebody else. Your mother and I always intended to bring a beautiful bride for you, a girl who would adapt to our ways. Our dreams have been shattered!' Father and son faced each other - the father seething with rage and the boy defiant. The boy stood his ground and threatened to leave home. The aggrieved parents finally relented.

The boy and girl were married in an extravagant ceremony, with their family and friends participating in the celebrations. Lyla made a beautiful bride, dressed in pale pink chiffon and the boy looked resplendent in traditional white *sherwani* and white turban. The faces of the couple glowed like candles in the dark. The father gave away his beloved daughter to the groom.

The honeymoon that followed was filled with sheer excitement and delight. They were euphoric - love exploded like fireworks, setting ablaze their horizon. Life stood at a standstill and they were enthralled in the moment with no yesterday and no tomorrow. They had chosen a special destination, a beach, where they lay all day on the sand and swam in the cool waters wholly possessed by each other.

And then, all too soon it was over and the ecstasy and euphoria subsided. They returned to set up a home independent of their parents. For the first year of their marriage the boy continued to lavish love and attention on his new wife and she continued to savour it. Then minor skirmishes erupted over limited finances, his frugal ways and his irascibility that would quickly explode into angst. The magic lamp was beginning to fade. The contempt of familiarity soured the relationship and the aura of the unfamiliar faded. Subliminal and restive emotions on both sides pushed to the surface and dormant skeletons awakened and vied for space. This turmoil brought out the worst in them.

Outwardly there was a calm of still waters as Lyla and her husband struggled, wanting to believe that issues would untangle by themselves. But the boy's inner demons were restless and broke away from their shackles, threatening to spill over. Increasingly, Lyla became his punching bag and the butt of his acerbic tongue. At first, she took things in her stride and refused to react. Lyla had been brought up in a cultured, calm home with fluid boundaries and a strong sense of gender equality. Small innocent pleasures gave her joy and she entertained no great ambitions. The boy was raised differently - he was ambitious and conniving and wanted control over his wife as affirmation of his manliness. His love was selfish and obsessive and he wanted to possess her body, mind and soul.

Lyla yearned to carve her own life and be in charge of herself. She was an artist who was looking for expression for her creative impulses to draw a special meaning from life. He was jealous of her art and resented that it drew her attention from him. For Lyla art was the essence of life. She converted a niche in their small house into a studio that became her sanctuary and an escape from the tensions and drudgery in the house. Here she worked arduously, putting in long hours, working on a beautiful painting of a woman nursing a baby. She perfected the soft contours of the woman with gentle brush strokes, with her supple body losing itself in the soft folds of the baby. The woman in the painting wore a pensive, melancholy look in her blue eyes. Lyla developed a special fondness for this picture. She could relate to its feminism, its melancholia and the intimacy with the baby. When it was finished, she took her husband to the studio and triumphantly pulled back the covering to reveal a stunning portrait. 'Look I made this painting. I have been working on it for six months now. How do you like it?' She was stricken by a cold look cutting through her.

'It's okay. It could have been better.' He shrugged his shoulders and left the room with complete indifference. His impassive face was a boulder of ice.

The following day she went to her studio to put the final touches to the painting. As she removed the covering, she was horrified to see the faces of the woman and baby smeared with black paint. Something broke inside her and she almost heard the thud of her fallen heart. She shook with rage, half-knowing who the culprit was - her husband! That evening when he came home, she confronted him. He was taken aback, went pale, but denied it, 'What are you talking about? I did no such thing! How dare you accuse me?' he growled.

Lyla almost lost her mind and shouted hysterically, 'You liar, I know you smeared the painting!'

He stepped back, then lunged forward and struck her on the face, 'How dare you call me a liar, you miserable wretch!'

The next day her paints and canvas went missing. She walked up to her husband, her anger rising, 'Now my paints and brushes are gone! What do you have to say to this?'

He turned crimson and shouted hoarsely, 'Get out of my house! Get out this instant, or I will throw you out! You have the audacity to point a finger at me!'

Lyla ran out of the house, tears streaming down her ashen face. She was stunned and her mind was frozen, spinning. She had been abused by the man she had adored, had defiantly married. His behaviour was a grave travesty of her love and faith in him. She could never forgive him. All her illusions came crashing down. Was she like millions of other women who were thrown out and abused by men whom they had trusted and vowed to love? Was love just a shallow stream, whistling a lustful song and then drying up? The road ahead was murky and her mind was bewildered, disoriented. The horizon loomed dark with black threatening clouds. Terror gripped her - she lost her balance and stumbled on the rocky, unpaved road.

NEVER LOOK BACK

From the hospital window he pointed to the sun setting on the horizon. 'Look darling, have you ever seen such a beautiful sunset on the California coast. It's breathtaking!' She looked at the setting sun he was pointing at, viewing the spectacular scene through his eyes. 'Look at those swirling clouds, grazing the horizon as the sun escapes from them and dips onto the earth.' Sophie stared at him incredulously and rejoiced at his jubilation. It was a relief to see him in this mood, after months of being bogged down by his debilitating disease.

That evening Sophie had left the hospital late, after having attended to all his physical needs. Just as she reached home, the phone rang, 'Yes, Sikander? Are you all right?'

'Yes, dearest, come immediately! I have something to share with you. Please hurry!'

Sophie protested, 'Sikander, I've just got back. Can't it wait until tomorrow?'

'I have no time left to waste. Please come quickly,' he replied with the same urgency. She frowned as she put the phone down. It was very unlike her husband to summon her so peremptorily, almost inconsiderately, she thought. Could his condition have worsened? With this in mind she picked up her bag and rushed out, speeding towards the hospital in a state of turmoil.

When she entered his room, she found him gazing out of the

window with a pensive look on his face. She stood there watching until, sensing her presence, he turned around. With a wave of his hand he beckoned her to come to the window and, holding her hand, pointed towards the sky. 'Sophie, look at the sunset. The sun is sliding into the deep red earth, spreading a million iridescent colours onto the sky! I couldn't bear not to share this with you. You can't miss these moments in life, they pass by too quickly.' Their eyes misted as they looked at each other for both knew that it might be the last sunset he would ever see.

That night he died. A few days later she buried him under a glowing setting sun. The sky had been overcast all day, but the sun had thrust its blushing face through the clouds just hours before the burial.

Sophie crumpled the tissue in her hand until it was reduced to thin shreds. She was haunted by memories racing through her mind. Sikander's extended illness had taken its toll and a chronic ache permeated every fibre of her being. She reminisced the day they had arrived in this country. He was dark and emaciated, his body slowly giving up on him as his kidney disorder worsened. 'Darling, I am doing this for you, since you wanted to come here. God give me energy to bear this displacement. Our friends and family are now far away but we still have each other,' he had said.

They had come to this beautiful country but life wasn't easy here. They moved in with their son and very soon he became a stranger to them. They were clearly a burden to him and his wife, but there was no going back. Decisions have a habit of plunging forward but never backwards, without redemption.

Then there was the final day of reckoning for the couple. Their son, Babur, spoke plainly and harshly, 'I am tired of supporting you. I can barely make ends meet for my family and myself. Either we leave or you must.' Flabbergasted, they quickly made alternative arrangements, rented a small apartment and moved out. That day they were truly heartbroken and blamed themselves for moving to the new country. It had brought them more stress rather than the better life they had anticipated. Sikander blamed Sophie, 'I told you it would be a wrong move, but you would not listen. You took this precipitous step that landed us here, and now we will have to pay for it. There is no going back! We have lost virtually everything.' There was a lengthy silence after which Sophie crept up to her man and whispered gently, 'We have each other and that is all that matters. Life has compensated us this way by bringing us closer to each other.' Their grief was softened as they embraced each other.

Sophie was able to secure a part-time job at the local school. The salary she earned was barely sufficient to support them, so they lived frugally, meeting only their basic needs. They were used to living simply since their earlier days when Sikander had been in the military service in Pakistan. They cooked simple meals at home, making do with plain clothing and cheap entertainment. Still they made it a point to have small vacations, on a beach or at a hill resort. Sikander loved the outdoors, away from crowds, relishing open spaces where the air was fresh and clean.

Sophie remembered one such day at the beach. It was warm and sunny and the waves were tranquil, embracing the shore and receding with frothing streaks. Sikander and Sophie had strolled on the sandy beach, the waves lapping their wet feet, making them sparkle. He looked much stronger since the time they had arrived here. Suddenly he had lifted her off her feet and carried her into the water. Laughingly he said, 'If only I had the energy of water, I would have carried you on the wave of eternity.' These were light-hearted moments for them, their cares forgotten.

There were other days when Sikander was cranky and irritable, stung by his inability to move on with life. His health was failing, and his agony became unbearable. He was inconsolable in those days and wept quietly. 'I am a sick man and am fed up with myself, and you just pretend to put up with me'. He had no appetite and pushed away the tray of food brought to him. Sophie was at her wits' end and desperately struggled to ease his suffering by tending to his every need.

As Sikander's health declined, his spirits ebbed. Then a heart attack weakened him further. He confided in Sophie, 'Dearest, my days are numbered, just a few weeks or months.' A distraught Sophie cried out, 'Hush, you must never utter these words! You're a resilient man and have survived many setbacks and emerged stronger. Just keep your spirits up, I beg of you.'

He continued in the same tone as if she had not spoken,

remembering his childhood days spent with his siblings. 'Omar was the mischievous one amongst the brothers and got into trouble in school until he was expelled. I remember the commotion in the house that day with father shouting and cursing, and mother in tears. And then he fled to Australia and never returned. My mother was heartbroken and never really got over it. Omar never returned their calls or letters and disappeared, as if he was never a part of the family. My father never forgave him, never softened his heart towards him, so great was his anger. Only I chose to stand up for him, but nobody listened. They never understood that I lost a part of myself in the only ally I had in the family.' Sophie listened quietly to him because she knew that at the end of the day, he had to clear his mind of all his nagging demons. It was his confession, a purgatory of sorts.

They talked of the death of their daughter, Marie. She was a perky girl with curly, black hair that tumbled over her face. Her father's pet, she would claim her place on her father's lap ahead of her siblings, 'I own him,' she would merrily laugh, while Sikander spoilt her with chocolates and candies. It was only when she suffered bouts of asthma did the light in her eyes fade away. It was heartbreaking to watch. Sophie was stoic though broken up inside and seldom revealed her distress. It was one of Sikander's greatest ordeals to see his darling daughter in pain. 'I can't bear to see Marie suffering. It breaks my heart. The disease has stolen her youth from her. I can't endure it,' he would moan.

There were many days when she was in hospital, her life precariously hanging between life and death. Then one day this sunny, bonny girl flew to her final abode, leaving them all heartbroken. Sikander didn't talk to anyone for days, shutting himself in his room. When he finally emerged from his room, his eyes were bloodshot but he didn't shed a tear. Only Sophie knew that his heart was torn apart. She could see many chapters of their life slowly closing, like the pages of a book. As the acceptance of the inevitable end grew, he would tell her, 'You must not grieve after I go. I know you will be lonely, but for my sake, find a man and get married. Your latter years should not be ravaged by loneliness.'

She listened to Sikander, and now this man with whom she had tied the marital knot stood next to her, reminding her of Sikander. The same build, tall and sturdy like a military man, a gentle profile, and just as determined and confident. He read her mind and spoke gently, 'Sophie you can't always live in the past. Memories, even if they are beautiful, metastasise with over-use, you cannot anchor your life on them.'

She looked at him for an instant and then her face crumbled, 'I caused his death. I brought him here to this country against his will. He never wanted to come, he said his life at home was comfortable amongst loving family and friends. He was a family man, full of love for everyone, always ready to help. Being away from them was like losing a limb. He couldn't take it for too long. He suffered and his spirit was broken.'

'You did no such thing, and even if you pushed him into coming here, you didn't cause his death. He was a sick man and his affliction was harsh and unrelenting. His body couldn't take it and he succumbed to his illness. Don't blame yourself, it isn't going to help you. Guilt is corrosive, it nibbles one's insides like a termite. Don't do this to yourself or to me, we don't deserve it.'

As she cried her heart out on his shoulder, he said quietly stroking her hair, 'Dead men have a way of leaving us quietly, dissolving like vapour.' As she wiped her eyes and smiled, he heaved a sigh of relief, 'There's my good girl! Strange are the ways of life, it gives as it takes. We have each other now.' At this moment she looked up and was startled to see the sun dropping over the soft skyline, whole and complete, ominously beautiful as always.

PREQUEL TO SISTER FRANCIS

Victoria was the fourth child in a Goan household. Every time her mother, Sylvia, became pregnant there was an air of suspense in the house as all hoped that a boy would be born. The house would be decorated with everything blue, balloons and all else in one hue. But each time the arrival of a baby girl would be met with gloom by Sylvia's husband, Victor.

When Victoria arrived, Victor lost his temper, 'Another girl! I am a very unfortunate man indeed!' And with that he stormed out of the house. Gloom again descended on the household. Sylvia was quiet and the other children clung to each other in fear. At night Victor returned and refused to talk to anyone. He was a strange brooding man who could not come to terms with the birth of another girl. Unlike his gentle, educated wife, Victor was bellicose and whipped up a storm in every situation, good or bad. Meanwhile, Victoria slept in her crib, defiantly peaceful. Sylvia's heart went out for the little baby who was rejected at birth by her father. Victor could not break away from the belief that girls were a burden and a curse in a home.

Victoria grew into a charming girl with curly black hair and a pale complexion. She had sharp features, a prominent nose, narrow piercing eyes and thin wide lips that broke into an impish grin. She was a vivacious child with exuberant energy. The four sisters, Stephanie, Cindy, Celia and Victoria, were raised in a strict Catholic home where religion played a significant role in moulding their lives. On Sundays the four little girls, dressed in pink dresses with their can-cans, were the picture of happiness. With their hair braided and tied with pink ribbons, they walked obediently to church. Only Victoria, with her exceptional energy, would break rank and run ahead of her older sisters. Her father would call out in a loud booming voice, 'Victoria! Don't run ahead, come back, you disobedient girl!' Victoria winced but showed no emotion, holding her chin up. She seethed inwardly and resented her father for targeting her. It was the norm with him and she never got accustomed to it. His constant reprimands and rebukes made her feel small and worthless. A shiver ran down her spine and she felt drained.

Victoria's growing years were coloured with strange sadness, a feeling of being unloved, unwanted and lonely - for the simple reason that she was a girl. She was the final arrival who was meant to be a boy. Ignoring her good qualities, her father missed no opportunity to belittle her. The slightest error on her part met with a sharp rebuke. 'You silly girl, your behaviour is highly reproachable!' Her confidence was severely shaken and she suffered bouts of depression.

Looking at herself in the gilded mirror in her bedroom, she could see a charming girl, long almond shaped eyes, a sharp aquiline nose and a strong chin. She could see no flaw in her face. She was acutely sensitive to the feelings of people around her and was aware of her unique ability to see them for what they were truly like under their outer façades. She curled her thin lips and looked defiantly into the mirror. 'I will show the world that I am not worthless. I will prove it to all of them until they are forced to acknowledge it,' she murmured.

It was in her mother's eyes that she saw the soft glow of compassion. When she was tired and disheartened, she crept into her mother's bed and lying there next to her warm body she would feel a sense of calm.

'Mother, you do love me, don't you?' she asked softly.

'Of course I do darling, how can you ever doubt that? You are my flesh and blood, an extension of me.' Victoria felt an immense relief, and though her mind challenged it, she wanted to believe it. Her heart ached to be loved.

Victoria was the cleverest among her sisters, energy spilling out of her like effervescent bubbles. A quick learner, she honed her skills, a mix of sciences and social arts. Her teachers complimented her, 'Victoria is an all-rounder with exceptional ability to learn whatever she sets her mind on.' She was driven by an intense desire to excel, not satisfied with doing less than her best.

Once her father summoned her and with a stern voice rebuked her, 'I have seen of late, Victoria, that you crave success far beyond your worth. Do you think girls were born to be high achievers? They are meant to play their domestic roles and not compete with men.' Victoria's heart sank and she felt that she was being pushed over the edge. She must stand on her own feet, even if it meant standing alone. Now more than ever she realised she was born with a mission, though she did not know what that was. She knew she had to validate her existence to the whole world.

One day, when she had escaped into their garden and sought refuge amongst the rows of roses and hyacinths from the humdrum of her daily life, she was spotted by her mother. 'Why, Victoria darling, what are you doing here?' she asked. 'Why this woebegone expression on your pretty face, darling?'

Victoria suddenly became overcome with emotion and cried, 'Oh Mother! Help me, help me! I am plagued by black moods that hang over me like dark clouds. I am confused and am looking for direction in my life, but the path is hidden in a fog. What shall I do Mother?'

Sylvia held her daughter tightly in her arms, 'Dearest, you are an exceptional child. Believe in yourself and you will one day find your way. Don't let anybody push or harass you, and God in his benevolence will show you the light.' Around them the day was fading and quiet descended. Gently Sylvia held her young daughter's hand and the two walked into the brightly lit house where the other girls were chatting and laughing over tea.

Victoria was closest to her sister Celia with whom she had developed a deep bond. Celia was a gentle, soft-spoken girl, quite the opposite of Victoria in both temperament and looks, and her quiet and subdued manner kept her away from their father's wrath. Over the years she had woven a shell of contentment, finding solace deep within herself. When the going got rough, the sisters cuddled with each other in the room they shared. Celia would say, 'Today, Victoria, I will read to you *Gulliver's Travels*. Those faraway lands fascinate me, they are like a dream I know will not turn into reality. Our lives are far too restricted to ever touch faraway shores, so let's enjoy reading about these lands.' Fiercely protective of each other, they joined hands against the powers over which they had no control.

Victoria turned eighteen and Christmas was round the corner. A Christmas tree stood in the living room decorated with brightly coloured lights. The air filled with revelry as Victoria's spirits were lifted by the festivities. A festive party was thrown for relatives and friends on Christmas Eve. This was the biggest celebration of the year and on this special day the elders also let down their reserve and had fun. A wooden floor was prepared for dancing. Victoria danced and flirted with boys, looking lovely in a flaming red dress. She was the centre of attention and her vanity was vetted by the special attention she got from them. 'Victoria it is my turn now to dance with you,' cried David, a handsome young man who was more special than all the other boys who hovered around her. He pursued Victoria, but marriage never really appealed to her, and in her mind, it was the most complex of all relationships. She thought that she wouldn't be able to bear to be hurt by a loved one. Either she must love with all intensity she could evoke, or she would remain aloof and solitary. She knew she dwelt on things too hard and too long, and in this way she was different from other girls her age. Those friends of hers - Emily, Josephine and all the others - were flippant and light-headed and dreamt of marriage. She shivered at the thought of a man touching her body, intimacy was anathema to her.

Tonight she danced with energy that flowed out in magnetic waves.

Finally, towards the end, she collapsed with fatigue. It was then that she saw her father watching her angrily from the corner of his eye. He was glowering like a demon and before she could react, he turned his head and walked stiffly away. He had once again thrown a dampener on a lovely evening. Her heart was full of foreboding.

The following day was Christmas and the family dressed in their best clothes and went to the local church to attend the morning service. Victoria walked morosely with her head down, recalling the episode of the previous day. She distanced herself from her father, lest he spoil the day with his ire as he had the previous night. With a heavy heart, she dragged her long legs to church. Once inside they ran to occupy their usual place with impatience. It was chilly inside and a draught was blowing from the open doors creaking in the wind. The priest started reading the sermon but she was barely listening and her mind was distracted.

Suddenly she was riveted to what the priest was saying, 'We are the children of Jesus and he loves each one of us more than a million fathers and mothers. Our soul is one with Him.' Victoria felt a searing pang and she touched her pounding heart. Her soul ached for the love of God, and she yearned to stay in His house forever. Suddenly she was enthralled in ecstasy, as if a physical force had poured a bucketful of love into her heart. Happiness splurged from every pore of her being, as if Jesus Christ had anointed her soul. Finally, she had found salvation in this quiet place that might prove to be her future sanctuary. It was then that the revelation struck her, like lightning from a dark sky, that she was destined to live in the warm, soothing and protective cloisters of the church. This was her mission that had haunted her in her days and nights. She knew at the back of her mind that she had always known that her destiny lay here.

When Victoria announced to her parents that she wanted to join the order and become a nun, they were stunned. Her father burst out angrily, 'Must you always act like a rebellious child! You know you will not be able take it for a day. And then you will shame us again by coming back!' With these cruel words he stormed out of the room.

Sylvia burst into tears, 'My darling child it is not an easy life, you will be giving up your family and everything else you have known in this life. Beyond doubt it is an honourable life, but I am not strong enough for this great sacrifice. I will not be able to bear the pain of your separation. I have already endured more than my share in life.' Victoria stared at her, surprised that her quiet mother was indirectly divulging for the first time what could be a painful secret that she had for years buried inside her. She was startled to see in front of her a haggard-looking woman with deep lines etched into her face and eyes that glowed embers. She had suffered and endured in silence all these years. Perhaps she had done it to keep her family together. At the end of the day did she regret her decision, no one would ever know. Victoria could put herself in her shoes at this moment and feel her pain, the same gnawing pain that she had lived with all her growing years.

Celia was in tears, 'How will I survive without you, it was your unrelenting humour that kept me from falling apart.' She paused for a while, deep in thought, 'I think I may follow in your footsteps before long.'

Victoria stood her ground amidst the uproar in her household. They were jolted, like an earthquake, and for the first time their perspective of each other had morphed into something unknown and unexpected. A member of the house was leaving them forever. Desolation filled them, forcing them to look inwards. Were they in any way complicit in this situation? But there was no turning the clock back and time had to move on. Victor, as was the norm, could not handle it, and it was unclear to Victoria whether he despised her more now or merely continued to burn in his own fire. She would never know, neither did she really care. She knew that whatever he did now could not make up for the pain that she had suffered at his hands and which could not be erased with an apology. She looked into the future with a quivering heart, the past better left forgotten like the fading glow of the setting sun.

Victoria entered the convent a month later and thus began the metamorphosis of this young woman. Her resolve grew with time and became as strong as a rock. Gradually the pain she endured in her adolescent years faded, and its place was filled light and love. A year later Celia joined the convent, finding her own peace. The two sisters were destined to be soul mates, sharing a vision all of their own. At the end of the day, they embraced their new life.

SISTER FRANCIS

The day finally arrived when Sister Francis was ready to take her solemn and final vows of chastity, poverty and obedience. It was an electrifying moment, the culmination of a long road to fulfilling her journey to becoming a nun and dedicating her life to the service of God. The journey had started the day Victoria had announced to her family her decision to enter a convent, and thus embarked on a path that was her destiny.

As a novice nun, Victoria had taken her vows and been baptised after the Saint Francis, also known as San Francesco of Assisi. Born in the twelfth century in Italy, he nursed the poor and sick at the risk of his own health, preached sermons to animals who rallied round him and eulogised all creatures as brothers and sisters living under God's umbrella. To the young Victoria he was a symbol of love that unites all beings under a celestial shelter.

In the early days Victoria struggled to adapt to the daily rituals of the convent. The regimen was strict and harsh and it was not easy for her wayward, wild nature. But change she must as she had set her mind to it. There were no choices here in the convent, there was only one path. Sorely tested, her spirit writhed and twisted amidst the hard-wired codes of discipline. She was told by the sisters, 'Conformity is the rule here. It is not a place where one can give in to one's natural impulses. Here you will traverse a narrow, well-chartered path, with signposts at every corner. Read them very carefully and obey. Here in the convent, it's your choice whether you choose to be happy or unhappy.' Victoria flexed her mind and prepared herself for the long road ahead and ardently prayed she would be able to meet the challenges she would undoubtedly face. She missed her home and longingly reminisced about the days spent with her siblings. She missed her mother who stood for everything positive and kept the family together under her wing. And then there was her father who lived a life of affliction and couldn't come to terms with his situation.

One day, to her utter delight, her mother came to visit her. She looked withered and sallow, her eyes were smudged and they had lost their light somewhere in the restive milieu that surrounded her. 'How are you, my darling Victoria? Oh! I miss you so much, my darling.' Sylvia's voice broke and her lean body shook.

'I am doing fine mother, don't fret about me,' she said stoically. She longed to tell her mother how she missed her warm embrace, her soothing voice, but she held herself back.

That was the last time she saw her mother. A year later her father called to tell Victoria that her mother had died. 'We buried your mother yesterday. You broke her heart when you left, and you, Victoria, you alone, are the cause of her death.' Then the phone went dead. No word of sorrow or consolation was spoken. Victoria cried all night and this time her grief was inconsolable. She knew that her painful past was buried with her beloved mother's mortal remains and now only memories remained to haunt her. There was no closure, no funeral to attend, no outburst of emotion, only a stifled cry, held in captivity for a lifetime.

In the privacy of her small cubicle, she confided to another novice nun, Sister Paul. 'I miss my family. I wonder if they ever think of me or have forgotten me like a fantasy from the past. Life after mother's death will not be easy, but I think I can cope because I'm a stronger person now.' Here her voice quivered and she gulped down her tears.

She was surprised when Sister Paul's eyes filled with tears. 'I can feel your grief, Sister Francis, for I am, sadly, in the same boat as you. I too am miserable here. My parents loved and pampered me since I was the eldest in the family. I miss them all so much, especially at night, when I cry myself to sleep. My family never wanted me to come here, but our local pastor, a very zealous man, cajoled me into it. I was intrigued by the world inside the convent. And then the only man I have ever loved, his name was Robin, jilted me and broke my heart. There was never anybody except him and I felt I had lost everything. I picked up the broken shards of my life and entered the convent. I guess, now that I am in here, I miss the vibrancy and energy of the outer world. I guess we can never have both sides of the world, these perimeters cannot be crossed,' Sister Paul lamented in a wild torrent of words.

'Oh! I am so sorry for you Sister Paul,' Francis's voice was full of compassion. 'I never knew you were so miserable. Believe me Sister Paul,' she said earnestly, 'with time you will begin to like this place, there is something magical about it. The hymns we sang today captured my heart and brought me close to Jesus.'

Sister Paul continued to cry and furiously wipe her red swollen eyes, 'I am not like you Sister Francis. You are so strong and together, I envy you.'

That night, though it was against the rules and was a severe breach of discipline, Sister Francis crept into Sister Paul's bed and stayed with her through the night. Her heart went out to the young girl who looked miserable and confused. She did not tell her own story, of her unloved existence, of the pain she suffered at home at the hands of her father. Now with her mother dead, the last thread of her childhood had broken. In contrast to her, Sister Paul had been raised in a loving happy home. No wonder she was dejected and lonely here. The intimacy of home was sorely missing in these walls.

The two novice nuns bonded over time, like siblings. Sister Francis was with her all through her emotional highs and lows. The distressed young girl suffered through a traumatic phase and had a nervous breakdown. Through the long nights she would sob, 'I miss my father and mother terribly and their loving embraces and kisses that I grew up with. I took it all for granted and never realised how fortunate I was.' Sister Francis was silent and could not help thinking of her own childhood. Her heart bled for her friend.

With the passage of time, Sister Paul broke loose from her childhood bonds, took her vows of Confirmation, and immersed herself in the sanctum of the convent. She knew if it were not for Sister Francis, who was the gentle dove who delivered letters of solace to her every day, she could never have made it. She wrote once, 'Dearest Sister Paul, be assured things have a way of resolving themselves with time. Soon you will fall in love with the peace and quiet of this place and will forget your past as it never happened. We are born with a mission and this is our destiny now. In place of our families we have the Lord Jesus to comfort us and give solace. Through meditation we will climb his threshold and find serenity within ourselves, a peace that is not in the humdrum lives outside the convent. They have their own struggles and strife to deal with. This place is now our sanctuary and our home.'

Sister Francis began to tutor young girls in the convent, who were full of ideals, dreaming of holding the world in their hands. She could see the first flame of ambition in their glowing eyes and could connect it with her own. Dreams of young minds were like fires burning in the wild. It was in that light that she saw many possibilities lying deep inside them. She never gave up on anyone, albeit the indolent girls were irritants in her eye, compelling her to lash out, 'You lazy girls! I will not and cannot tolerate tardiness.' But she knew better than to break their spirit. She would later summon the erring youngsters to her office, which was a small, sparsely furnished room with an unpolished wooden chair and table. Her empathy put a light back into the young girls' eyes. 'You know, my children, I see potential in you and my heart grieves to see you waste your talent. Later in life you will regret these years you so foolishly squandered but then it will be too late.' When she saw the remorseful look on the girl's faces, she hugged them, 'Children! Do not fear, I will be at your side whenever you need me.' She herself was stunned to see the difference it made in later years, when the same girls blossomed into successful women. She was right in treating every child as a tool which she must polish to a point, pushing not too hard nor too leniently.

It was a galaxy of girls who flitted through the corridors of the convent like multiple iridescent images and they stayed with her. They were printed on her canvas and became a part of her being. By helping these girls, she had in some way healed herself and they sutured the broken strands of her life. Their youthfulness spilled over into her and she was young again.

Oftentimes her girls would stealthily creep into the small wood-panelled library to chat with her. As they happily snuggled up to her they would say, 'Sister, please let's read Shakespeare's Julius Caesar together. As she read, the girls learnt the power of the great classics, how life could be done and undone in a fraction, or the sudden metamorphoses of people under life's catastrophes. Hamlet, Othello, Richard III depicted an ugly starkness of the power men had wielded through the ages, over hapless, marginalised beings, mostly women and children. This was the kind of world they would one day inhabit and struggle in unknowingly. She prayed for their safety.

Sister Francis knew her life had not been out of the ordinary. In the solitary nights, she felt a lingering wound in her heart, still sore and tender. A flashback of painful moments haunted her, when her father's stern voice would bear down on her in her dreams, constantly rebuking and belittling her. That nightmare never left her.

When Sister Francis announced to her students that she was relocating from Lahore to the bustling city of Karachi, the girls were devastated. They protested and pleaded with her to stay. One day coming down the winding steps she heard a plaintive voice behind her. It was Salha! 'Please stop, Sister Francis! I have something to say,' cried the girl breathlessly.

Sister Francis paused and looked up gently at her, 'Yes, my dear, what is it?' She knew there was something wrong. This girl had a special place in her heart.

She was sobbing now, 'Sister I beg you not to go. It is our final year in the convent. Surely you can't desert us now! Our performance in tests will decline!' Sister's heart softened towards the young Salha, who looked so sad and defenseless. Sister Francis sat down on the steps and pulled the girl towards her. Tears rolled down Salha's tear stained face.

Sister Francis took her hand and said, 'Don't cry darling, you must know I can't stay. We in the convent are God's humble servants and must go wherever, whenever we are beckoned. And please remember, no one in life is indispensable, people will come and go, and life moves on. You should try not to get too attached to anyone, people will be fickle and ruthless at every turn, just as there will always be people standing by you.' They sat holding hands till Salha's sobbing subsided. Sister Francis pressed her hand warmly and gently let her go. Then she rose and walked down the corridor, a tall, stately woman in a long white habit, with a firm and strident gait, her backbone upright like a sole warrior. At that moment Salha knew Sister Francis would not be returning, but also realised that she had organically delivered a vital message that would stay with her.

In her later years, Sister Francis received a stellar award. The audience at the ceremony held at the Governor's House knew nobody deserved it more than her. Her contribution in the field of education spanned many decades. The state governor who handed the award said to her, 'Sister Francis, this is a happy moment for me as well, for my daughter was your pupil and she adored you with all her heart. It is my pleasure and honour meeting you today as I have the opportunity to thank you. Do you mind if I ask you a question? How did you win the hearts and minds of all those thousands of girls?' Sister smiled and replied, 'Thank you, Sir, for giving me this honour. I don't know how I won the hearts of all my girls, for I am a humble servant of God who loves his creations.' At that moment there was not a single man or woman in the audience whose eyes were not wet. Only Sister Francis remained calm and composed, like an intrepid soldier on a battlefield. She had endured much in life and knew how to hold herself with great dignity. She could not complain, life had given her more than she could have ever imagined. She, on her side, had given as much of herself to life. It had been a fruitful odyssey, replete with fulfilment and full of heartaches. She had carved her life the way she wanted. She had the best of both worlds, the life in the convent and outside. She had accomplished this through sheer unrelenting will and energy, her magic being she had never ceased to hope.

In all those years her life was sheltered within the walls of the convent, Sister Francis had not denied herself the pleasures of art, music, theatre and films and was a regular visitor to these places with sister nuns and young students. The girls were her compatriots and she counselled them daily, for her concerns for them lay beyond the convent. 'Embrace life fully, as the birds embrace the skies. Otherwise you will end up stumped by fear.' She knew the world outside and feared for them, and told them earnestly, 'Never create distances between people with intent of racist leanings, it is demeaning, a terrible closure of hearts and minds. The world is too rich a place to shut oneself into tight compartments. The milieus you will inhabit outside will later change you in many ways, but you will always carry these precious treasures of learning as you cross the many milestones in your life.' She was their lifetime mentor and they would never forget her.

The years flew in a flash and it was finally time for her to retire, leaving Karachi for a small village in rural Punjab. She confided in her sister nun, Sister Clarence, 'It is with a heavy heart that I retire from active life. I will miss the city of Karachi with its brisk-paced life. Of course, I was never an active part of it but my soul savoured vicariously its many flavours and iridescent colours.' She smiled faintly, her eyes glowing, 'But then I will not complain, God has been good to me. I am about to enter another phase in my life and I must move forwards and not look backwards.' She waved her frail hand lightly, 'I am at peace now, a pilgrim who has reached her journey's end.'

Sister Clarence, one of her close companions, said reassuringly, 'Sister Francis you will continue to be a beacon of light wherever you go.'

Sister Francis had a faraway look in her eyes. She was elsewhere and not listening.

SONNY'S DILEMNA

A woman was sitting on the couch in her lounge, focusing on the pile of newspapers spread out before her. She had the habit of immersing herself deeply in them on most days. This was her link to the world outside; this was where she sifted reality from fiction, to fuel her mind and to keep her sanity. Meditatively, she soaked in the stillness in the room which was bereft of human touch - of gregarious laughter or light banter.

The woman's son walked in and out of the room, shuffling his feet, seeking her attention, and yet biding his time. Finally, she looked up, spectacles hooked on her long, straight nose, 'Sonny, do you have anything to say to me? I can hear your uneasy footsteps.'

Sonny, a lanky boy, with a nose like a cragged ledge, jaw set tight, replied, 'Nothing really, mother, I just wanted to tell you that I am going hiking with friends for a week.'

She paused a moment before replying, 'Have I ever stopped you from going anywhere? I will miss you, but I will not stop you from going.'

The boy shifted uneasily on one foot then another. He considered his mother's reply to be a veiled statement that held him captive emotionally and yet released him physically. 'Can I take this as consent?' he asked hesitantly, catching his breath between words.

'Sonny, don't try to trip me on my words. I have given my

consent to you to go with your friends. I can see that being with them is more important than spending time with a boring old woman, even though she happens to be your mother.' Sonny opened his mouth, and then clamped it shut, thinking the better of it, and left the room, his feet heavy on the wooden floor.

'Don't drag your feet. The sound grates on my nerves!'

The woman stared at the receding back of her son and continued to turn the pages of a newspaper as if there had been no intervention, immersing herself deep into its flesh. The newspaper was meat that she devoured and digested with the slow churning of her stomach. It pumped her circulation, bolstered her intellect and spun her mind into action.

The woman's husband had died in an air crash many years ago, when Sonny was only a toddler. It was sudden and devastating, numbing her spirit and leaving her devastated. During their years together she had lapped up his wealth, lived in luxury and never had to soil her hands with regular domestic drudge. She didn't need to do much thinking either, as decisions were taken and executed by him. He loved her, had stood by her, steadfast in his love, and greater so in his loyalty.

She bore him a son, a handsome bonny baby, resembling his father. The father doted on the boy, being given to loving intensely as was his nature. The child was his gift from God and he treasured him. He wanted to give him everything he could and his wife went along with him.

After his death, his dreams for the boy stood like an unfinished agenda. She did not have the vision or the will to carry them forward. She left it to God and to fate, that inexorable spectre that validated even death. The woman dressed the boy in his father's image and silently pledged her loyalty to him. She hung her husband's portrait on the wall alongside that of her son, thereby resurrecting her dead husband, and she prayed daily for him and the boy. Her strong faith in God gave her strength.

When Sonny returned from his week-long vacation his mother was ecstatic, fussing over him, feeding him *halwa* and *kheer*, chatting excitedly, giving him updates on the latest news, the neighbours' usual misdemeanours and their rowdiness. The boy briefed her about his activities. He had trekked a rugged terrain, camped on a hillside and had eaten with and met with locals of the area. They were poor people, living at subsistence level, but happy in their small world. They were excitedly communicative, relating folklore and stories dating back several centuries.

When the excitement ebbed, mother and son fell into their old routine. It was evening and light was fading outside. Inside the house there was quiet and both were preoccupied in their separate activities. The mother was darning Sonny's socks, and complaining at the same time, 'Sonny, how do you wear your socks? They look as if you tear them up daily. And your trousers are tattered, all in one trip. When will you grow up, son?'

Sonny sat clutching his laptop as if it was a precious baby and heard her vaguely. He set his laptop aside only when he went to the kitchen to make himself a cup of tea. He downed many cups of tea in a single day, an addiction that kept him going and made him think straight on good and bad days. On most days, however, the mother and son did not have much to say to one another. The boy, being reticent, had locked his feelings inside him, fearing that if they strayed, he would be exposed to his mother's strict vigilantism. His mother, likewise, was not inclined to share things with him, except of a practical nature. These were tasks that were to be done inside and outside the house, like grocery shopping, paying monthly bills and upkeep of the house. Perhaps she did not share because she considered her son to be immature. She preferred instead to read the newspapers or watch television as this enabled her to move outside of herself, without upsetting the applecart.

Ensconced in their own spheres, they did not always see eye to eye. He lived life in moments and she dwelt in the multiple phases of her life. He was on the threshold of a novel transitory flight, ready to take off, whilst she was couched in a comfortable niche, carved by life's experiences. Any argument between them would end by the mother saying, 'Son, listen to me, I have a whole wealth of experience on my plate, whereas your plate is empty.'

Suddenly the bell rang. It was the neighbour's son, 'Have you seen my cat? She wandered away today and hasn't come back. I thought she might have sneaked in here.' The boy, a bonny, bright-eyed child with a fixed smile on his face, marched in with gusto.

The woman was energized and cried out, 'No, I haven't seen her today, she must have strayed elsewhere.' Then on a friendly note she said, 'Since you have come in, have a piece of cake that I baked today.' The boy's face lit up and he joyfully came up to her. She brought the cake from the kitchen, cut a generous slice, and gave it to the boy. 'Come here boy, tell me what you are doing these days. I have missed you, you must come and visit me often, you know, old people have no one to talk to. Of course Sonny is here, but we need more company.' The boy buoyantly narrated small incidents, stories of the neighbour's dog wreaking havoc on their doormat, and the fights between cats and dogs in the street. Then having downed the cake greedily, he made a gesture to leave. The woman waved her hand, 'Give my love to your mother and come again.' All this while Sonny stood aside, like a bystander, watching his mother's mood swings. When the boy left, the woman and Sonny resumed their solitary activities, and silence continued to fall tirelessly, like a dark night.

Sonny looked at his mother at intervals and saw her furrowed brow and distracted look. This upset him. He wanted to move closer to her and embrace her, yet he feared that if he ever ventured to make a drastic move he would embarrass her and she might pull away on some pretext. The pretence did not go away - she wanted him to grow up and act like a man, and he wanted to be her child and be cuddled by her. Neither was attuned to the other's needs. She was a cold, self-centered woman, aloof in many ways, and he was a confused boy who never really understood his mother.

Then one day the bubble burst. Sonny had been applying to colleges in other cities. He received a letter of acceptance from one of the best colleges in a big city. He was beside himself with joy. He ran to his mother to break the good news. There was pin drop silence before she spoke. 'Congratulations, my son. This is a test of your merit. But, of course, you can't go, you can study in our city, it has many good colleges.'

Sonny was momentarily tongue-tied and then he spoke, 'Mother, this is the opportunity of a lifetime. If I miss this, I will never get another chance. I will not be gone for good. After graduation I will come back. Time will fly!'

At this moment, the woman flew off the handle. She clenched her teeth, cried in a hoarse, piercing voice, 'Have I raised you for this day, that you should abandon me? I have laboured night and day to nurture you single-handedly, through agonising nights when you were ill and feverish. Is this the gratitude I get for my pains?'

Sonny was speechless. He cowered, unprepared for this outburst. He had wanted to give her a surprise, thinking she would be happy for him. He could not understand her reaction. Did she not love him enough to let him go? Until today he felt shackled by her for even trivial freedoms that he wanted. She corrected him always: 'Don't walk in a slovenly way' and 'Hold your chin up, be a man.' She made him think he lacked guts. She would oftentimes throw in his face, 'I stood up to all misfortunes after your father's death. I handled the family estate, I faced opposition from relatives - it is a man's world, and they didn't like that I had guts. Women who are lone fighters are mocked by men and told that they should know their place in society. But God was on my side and with His blessings I won my battles. I knew that I had you, and I didn't think I would ever lose you.'

That day, after his mother's outburst, Sonny made up his mind. He would leave, go to college and use the money she had kept aside for him. He would not tell her as she would be heartbroken, but she would heal with time and come to terms with it. She had always been a survivor. Sonny was soft-hearted and did not want to hurt her. He slipped away in the wee hours of the morning with no idea when he would return. He was in no mood to ponder over it and he would think about it another time, another day.

The woman woke the next day, searched the house, and not finding Sonny, saw the writing on the wall. He had left the house secretly, without telling her. Her mind looked for answers, but her narcissistic mind, usually foggy, was swept by self-pity. She was aware of a deep pain piercing her insides, knowing she had lost the only person who mattered in her life. She knew she could not hold on to her son forever and wondered forlornly where she had gone wrong. She put aside the newspaper, rose, straightened her hunched shoulders, walked to her bedroom and went to sleep. The stillness around her was deafening today. She was convinced that life was becoming more erratic as she aged. She must now attempt to embrace the turbulence in her raging heart. By tomorrow she would feel better, having pieced together the broken slivers of her heart and seen the light at the end of the tunnel.

THE BOY WHO RAN AWAY

On a cold winter morning the woman sat in a restaurant sipping hot coffee and eating croissants. The place was bustling with people, mostly young people engrossed in their laptops. At another table close by a boy and girl were engaged in conversation, not intimately but attentively. They seemed to be second-generation immigrants. The woman was taken in by the boy's resemblance to a relative from her younger days. This boy had the same large eyes, thick eyelashes, wide but thin lips, broad smile and long shapely nose tilted at the edge like a T-junction. He might even be the son of her long-lost cousin. She observed that the boy talked with ease in low tones while the girl listened attentively. He talked glibly to impress the girl. From what the woman could gather from pieces of the conversation that she overheard, he was narrating anecdotes from his past.

Forty years ago the woman's cousin had left home and come to the USA for a better life. His family back home had lived in near poverty, and his mother had struggled to feed her large family. The father came from an old established family but had fallen on hard times and had eventually retired with a meagre pension. He remained a jolly, light-hearted fellow, even in his hour of trial. In the evenings he would regale the family with stories of his childhood, tales of comedy and tribulation, peppered with twists of humour told with a sober face. The children enjoyed these evening tales. This was when they felt loved and united as a family. However, hungry mouths became disgruntled over time and love alone could not hold them together. There was constant friction in the house. The parents, who doted on the children, were dismayed to see the family falling apart.

The father had a special spot for his two daughters who were both talented and pretty. The girls were ambitious and did well for themselves. One joined the coveted profession of medicine and multiplied her assets, and the other married a handsome, well-to-do man from a good family, whom she loved dearly. The three boys on the other hand hung loosely like wayward kites, and were unable to pull themselves out of the quagmire of doing nothing. They became disgruntled, consumed with anger and envy for their well-to-do distant relatives who enjoyed good fortune and offered no help to lift the family out of destitution. The boys, in desperation, were goaded by wild impetus to change the course of their lives.

Over time the boys distanced themselves from their nuclear family. They mocked their father for his failure in life and his apparent lack of concern for their well-being. On his part, the father's anger at the slothful existence of his sons was partially diffused by fatherly love. Their mother doted on them, was soft-hearted and lacked the iron will to discipline them. She let them be, letting them come into their own. And this they did.

The family fell victim to a series of misfortunes seemingly beyond their control. One son drowned at sea and his dead body was brought to their door by strangers. He was living a reckless life in one of the bigger cities and his death was also due to recklessness. He was not a good swimmer and yet he ventured far into the deep sea. He had drowned before he could be rescued. The parents were heartbroken to see their handsome boy cut down in the prime of life.

Grief had not yet abated when the younger daughter took her own life, impulsively, in a fit of rage and grief. The parents were shattered, the pretence of a happy, united family collapsed like a house of cards. It took a toll on their health and they became sickly and grew decrepit fast. The father continued reading stories in the evening light, many of them now a grim reflection of his own life. His fractured relationship with his own father, who had beaten him on many occasions, including when he had run away from school, came back to haunt him. His father had, in those times, pointed his finger at him and admonished him severely, 'You will always be a good-for-nothing and you will live to regret it!' Childhood memories reside in the innermost closets of the mind and appear in many forms. These took the form of stories, rumbling in his mind like half-forgotten fables.

The second sister was eccentric, abusing tradition and oscillating between a series of failed marriages. She refused to conform to common codes of conduct in life and moved into her atypical space where she dwelt alone. She worked hard and made a lot of money, but lost it as quickly. She bore two children to two husbands; one child turned to music and the second shunned conformity by declaring himself to be gay. She gave her parents financial support, as a son is expected to do, and thus eased their economic woes. But she was a restless soul leaving home periodically and like a nomad could not settle anywhere for long. She died early of natural causes but not without having abused her mental and physical health with her nonconforming ways.

The second son had an innate respect for tradition and married a woman who upheld whatever there was to hold in the way of values. He worked as a clerk in a local company, had two boys who were taught religion and conformity, and became sticklers to time-honoured values. He lived conservatively, while his wife served him and his family, maintaining the status quo and thus gaining the reputation of being an 'honourable' woman. They didn't strive to rise above mediocrity and thus remained safe from wanton eyes.

The youngest son was reckless and impetuous, somewhere between an idealist and a cynic. Being her favourite, his mother indulged his every wish. His father, on the other hand, considered him to be a loser and a wastrel, demeaning him at every opportunity. The boy didn't know where to turn in an unstable family, tottering between love and rejection. The father was agnostic and the mother practiced a rigid moral code while the children navigated an in-between path. The youngest boy could make nothing out of this mixed baggage. He had performed poorly at school and was told he had ADHD, something neither he nor his family understood. The boy's turmoil raged unabated. A close friend who lived on the same street showed him a way out and suggested they go west, where hope and prosperity beckoned. One night the two boys went missing and were gone for good. They never contacted their families again and the families gave up on them after a few years.

The woman, taking her last sip of coffee, knew that her cousin never returned home. It was a complete severance from the family. The years had rolled by and now this boy sitting at the other table seemed to be the copy of her cousin, and possibly could be his son. She observed that the boy was adept at advancing himself with the girl to create his special space. Clever young immigrant, she thought, quite typical also. His talk circled around himself whilst the girl listened, apparently liking his charming ways and not so transparent manner. Across the room the woman knew, being an immigrant herself, that dwellers in foreign lands carried a part of themselves closer to home in tight closets. The winds of change, lulling but hostile, blew around them but they stayed firm.

The woman rose, paused at their table and posed a question: 'Young man, you resemble a relative of mine who came to this country forty years ago and we never heard from him again. Are you from Pakistan and from the city of Hyderabad?'

The boy, unruffled, rolled his big eyes, and replied casually, 'No, somewhere between Lahore and Peshawar.'

The woman looked surprised. 'Maybe I made a mistake. Sorry, son,' she apologised and walked out of the restaurant onto the busy street. She wished she could have held his attention longer, but then she might have crossed barriers. She had found his answer evasive, but then the man who was her cousin had lived for years in anonymity and so had his family. Perhaps he, the lost generation, never found a foothold, swaying between hope, fear and despair. The second generation was better at surviving. They mingled better. She felt that at the end of the day, people are all extensions of each other some way or the other, whether they like it or not, and they hide their true identities in a world deemed hostile.

THE CHERRY BLOSSOM FESTIVAL

A gloriously radiant sun thrust itself through dark clouds on the morning of the Cherry Blossom Festival at Roosevelt Island, scattering luminous heat on an undulating land. On the ground the first tiny sprouts of green grass shyly turned up their faces. The city was galvanised with robust energy, flinging away its lazy, winter-mode mantle as people spilled out on to the streets. Sunshine and the prospect of viewing cherry blossoms transformed city folk into one vigorous, jubilant crowd.

The island hosting the festival at the onset of spring was transformed into one rolling sea of people. Walking leisurely, couples bonded with their children, boys and girls walked romantically hand in hand, clusters of giggling girls and energy-propelled groups of boys shed their daily workloads to embrace a light-hearted mood. On a daily basis the city's populace artfully juggled between work and play, changed gears, opened and shut their mind's vents to survive in an intensely competitive environment. If it had not been for the occasional indulgence in light pastimes they would be bogged down with fatigue. After all, they were actors, consciously or unconsciously struggling on in their own little islands.

On a platform in a corner were Japanese performing actors, dancing and singing. Music was their pathway to the soul, central to life, central to love, and had been so through the eons. Nearby, stalls under white canopies served Japanese teas, blends of their local flavours, soothing to both body and spirit. Here, on this island thronged white people, black people, brown people and yellow people, mingling into the crowd, yet holding their spots. Each one carried within a host of cultural mixes, part and parcel of their migrant stock and held on tightly to them. To relinquish them would be to lose oneself but with time, they became diluted, overlapped, sucked into homogeneity. Some morphed into appendages, others clung onto their past. The second generation was more astute. They were termed 'progressive'. The new order was liberal and endearing in its form, yet mercenary, unforgiving, and ruthless in its execution.

Here, on Roosevelt Island, a similar scene was being enacted. The Cherry Blossom Festival had disappointed the crowd, blossoms were sparse on dry, straggly trees. Spring was still nervously tottering on winter's edge, bashful and frugal. The crowd expected an abundance of cherry blossoms, trees pregnant with bounty, swaying in the wind. None of this was seen here. They shifted gears, turned to family and friends with attentive love, patiently queuing up in long lines for a sandwich or coffee. They did this with ease born out of long habit. They knew the importance of nurturing starved relationships stressed by daily life. This was a show of the great capacity of a city to offload, distract and rehydrate their spirits in quest of temporary calm.

And then it happened. A sea of people congregating from early morning turned into a colossal wave, gradually building momentum. A logjam at a security check unnerved an otherwise patient crowd. Someone struggled to break loose, triggered a push and heaved, and the crowd, like a breaker, rolled. A huge mass, like a predator, consumed hundreds of unsuspecting people. The crowd turned into a wild, frenzied mob. There were screams climaxing into hysteria, angry outbursts, violent protests, and a show of ruthless self-preservation. It was a do or die situation. Some pushed to rescue themselves, the elderly helplessly succumbed, and young men and women struggled. People were crushed underfoot, some seriously injured. In a moment the situation had spiraled out of control and the crowd had become a mob, turning violent. The crowd was running wildly, vicious emotions uncapped and naked.

Ambulances and the police arrived immediately to attend to the injured and to restore order to the frenzied scene. Rumours circulated that the subways had shut down and all vehicular traffic was blocked. People felt trapped and claustrophobic. The only route out was across a bridge connecting the island to the mainland. Dense crowds headed to the bridge a short distance away. They walked fast, some ran, as if chased by lost time.

Finally, the crowd hit the main road where cars and buses carried on as usual. The state of frenzy now abated, its heat evaporating. They heaved a sigh of relief as they finally slumped into buses, subways and taxis. An old lady, collapsing into a subway seat, muttered breathlessly, 'I am glad the nightmare is over. I can't believe I survived.' Her audience, sitting with pinched, tired faces, sighed.

An elderly gentleman's voice rose above the crowd, 'Cheers to the Cherry Blossom Festival, thank God it is over! What an anti-climax to a bright sunny day!' They shuddered and lapsed into silence.

Meanwhile the subway train glided into the dark tunnel, navigating towards known destinations of respite.

THE DAY DRAGGED ON

A man and a woman sat together watching television as it continuously transmitted shock waves of sensation-packed news, scenarios of wars, scandals and collapsing states. The world appeared to be coming to pieces. In the living room the scene was comical as the couple vegetated, starved of emotion, like two robots transfixed in a time capsule. Something had frozen inside them and they seemed to have morphed into two loveless beings detached from themselves and each other. The drifting away was a gradual process born of mutual neglect and cold indifference. It began at a point in time and then kept accelerating until it became a deep swamp from where there was little redemption.

The day dragged on, unnoticed, when nothing moved and if anything did, it was in a void of silence. The man casually switched channels until he settled on one of his favourites. The woman, tall, elegant and poised, not being able to take it anymore, rose and switched off the television, as if disengaging from an enemy. The man looked up at her with annoyance. 'Why have you turned it off? The suspense in the criminal proceedings of a corrupt politician was mounting, and now because of you, I have lost the thread of it all!'

The woman looked at him with thinly veiled contempt. 'You have been sitting here like a zombie all day and still you have not had enough of it. I must say, you have great stamina for inconsequential and irrelevant things in life. We have squandered our weekend, we could have dined out or gone to visit my aunt!'

The man looked at her tiredly and said, 'Well, what else would you have me do with my day? I get only one day off in a week and I want to spend it doing what I want to do, and there you go denying me my small pleasures. Your aunt is boring and anyway, she doesn't like me. Next time pay her a visit without me.'

The woman replied, 'You're only imagining that my aunt doesn't like you. You are a fairly straight guy with no objectionable traits. She might be somewhat judgmental, but then most elderly people are that way, so kindly make some concession for her. And as for denying you your small pleasures, you are welcome to savour them! But I can't help feeling sorry for you! All you do, day in and day out, is constantly watch television shows that churn out propaganda and intrigue. They are twisting the public mind and exposing it to a malaise, deep and brutal. You will become brain dead some day!' She heard a low grunt, but continued, 'You know, I believe that this feeds into a primal, vicious craving within you that needs to be slaked. And this I say is not only in your case, but it is feeding a deep-down brutal hunger in audiences globally as well.'

The man had heard enough, even with his mind half-closed, and rose abruptly from the sofa. 'You will always see the darker side of the picture. For heaven's sake, adjust your crooked lens. It is the social media of today that has lit the dark minds of the illiterate people in our country. But your ranting will never stop!'

The woman's face changed colour and turned pale, but she remained quiet, sensing danger, like a deer in the night. Words, like missiles, did more damage than good, she reminded herself.

The man paced restlessly in the living room, pretending to sort out artifacts that had been placed randomly on the tables. He then came back and sat down on the sofa again and switched on the television. His face was subdued like smudged colours in a painting. Suddenly, he became aware that he was grinding his teeth. The woman picked up a book and sat in a corner, holding on to her silence and peace.

The day had passed and nothing had changed, and the world remained as it was. Meanwhile the monster in the television continued to blast horror stories to a captive audience. A few decades from now, the effects of this addiction would magnify, becoming indistinguishable and indistinct from a mind stunted by age-old weathering.

THE DEBACLE

'Bibijan!' a voice resonated across the corridor. 'Where are you?'

The woman looked up from her embroidery and smiled in response. 'I am here, sweetheart,' she said but made no move to go to him, and remained seated in her comfortable wicker chair next to a table on which was a colourful bouquet of flowers. She loved roses in particular and never tired of breathing in their scent, which she did all day long. She was a fair complexioned woman with a curly crop of red, henna-dyed hair that wouldn't sit still on her head, perhaps because it was never combed. As a habit she would sit all day in the sunshine, however relentless the sun might be. Now she shaded her face with her hands from its slanting rays and looked up, smiling at her husband who was standing before her. Although they had been married for many years, she still felt joy in his company. He was a tall, lean man with a clean-shaven face which magnified his features. He had deep-set eyes and a firm jawline, but it was his prominent nose standing out like a craggy hill that dominated his face. He had a commanding voice like that of a military officer who knew his authority.

'Bibijan, I have news for you, but before that I must have my cup of tea. I can feel my blood sugar level falling.'

'Feroze!' he called out to his servant, 'Please bring our evening tea.'

The servant, who appeared in the door, answered, 'The kettle is already on the stove, Sir. I will just bring it.'

Feroze arrived with a silver tray carrying tea and biscuits and Jamshed waited for the servant to pour the tea. He then dismissed him with a wave of his hand. 'Now Bibijan, let me come to the point.'

Jamshed had never looked so serious in his life and Bibijan looked at him anxiously. Jamshed continued in a heavy voice, 'The riots in the city are escalating day by day. The insurgency is growing and a battalion of troops has arrived from West Pakistan to quell the separatist movement of the Mukti Bahini, the Bengali guerilla force. The battle is on and both sides are fiercely engaged in combat.'

'Oh my God!' Bibijan sat up, her face puckered with anxiety. 'Tell me, how serious is it? Are our lives in danger?'

Jamshed was quiet for a moment, his jaw jutting out, giving himself time to deliberate before he spoke again. 'For now, non-Bengalis are safe here, especially people like us who are in the employment of the Government of Pakistan. Bengalis want to secede and be independent for they are at the end of their tether. They have a host of unfulfilled grievances that have been festering for a long time. A case of poor governance by the state has killed the spirit of unity amongst its citizenry. Religion can no longer hold us together. And there is another piece of news: India is supporting the movement.'

'Why don't we go to Hyderabad Deccan? Mummy and Daddy will be only too happy to have us back. We can return when things settle.'

'Bibijan, try to understand. All my life I have worked in the Pakistan Civil Service and when I retire I will draw all my emoluments from Pakistan. Now if we move to India from Bengal I may lose everything and we will be paupers and dependent on your parents, something I will always detest.'

'So, are you saying we will have to go to West Pakistan and leave Dhaka for good, where we have spent many happy years of our married life and seen such wonderful days?' Bibijan said in dismay.

Jamshed waved his hands helplessly, 'As it is said, there is a tide in the affairs of men…This can pull us towards unknown destinations. All we can do is to follow it.'

Bibijan was crestfallen, but when she looked at her husband who was always courageous in the midst of storms but who now looked so worried, she said, 'I will be happy as long as we are together. I know we can make it together in West Pakistan.'

'That's good to hear!' Jamshed gave her an affectionate peck on her cheek, to which she responded with a loving smile. She was his first love and his last, and although they were poles apart in mind and spirit, they had developed a deep and abiding love that held them together through good times and bad. He had stood like a bulwark beside her and she basked in his strength. She knew she was difficult and demanding in many ways, but he never tired of indulging her small whims. She would sit outside in the garden the whole day while the chores of the house were performed by servants. He was accustomed to overseeing everything. She had in fact never needed to take on the burden of any responsibilities and lived a sheltered existence.

She had one passion in life and that was tennis. She excelled in the game and had won many medals which she displayed in an ornate glass cabinet in her living room. Nothing, not even her husband, could persuade her to give up playing even when she was pregnant with her children. She had miscarried several times, but made no compromises for her passion. Her husband grudgingly conceded to her desires. He loved her too much to let anything disturb the peace between them. Secretly he was fearful of her moods, for she was given to quick outbursts of temper which he found very upsetting. Fortunately, she was equally quick to calm down.

Jamshed would never forget the day his wife won her first medal, for like a loyal husband he had invested his time in his wife's sport. She had played at their favourite club and he sat in the front row, his face glowing with pride. She was dressed in white with a red scarf, looking prettier than ever, even if slightly tomboyish. She dealt swift strokes adeptly and was winning every point against her opponent. The crowd was jubilant and cheered her on, with Jamshed's applause being the loudest. He stood and cheered her as she walked to the podium after her decisive win. Bibijan had been overcome with emotion by the thunderous applause. Much to his surprise, she beckoned him to join her and she held his hand as she shouted, 'Here is the man who deserves this award as much as I do. If it was not for his unconditional support I wouldn't be here today.' These words were the most precious gift she had given him.

Those were wonderful days for the couple in East Pakistan. Jamshed was an astute civil servant and was respected for his integrity and commitment to work. They lived in a sprawling old colonial house where they entertained lavishly. The food and company at these parties was exceptional. The men segregated from women and discussed politics and the tensions brewing between the East and West wings of the country. The Bengalis were disgruntled, but usually a cordial atmosphere prevailed at these gatherings. The women, some more fearful than others about the deteriorating situation, sat together and were engrossed in similar discussions. Yet the women had the tendency to lean towards hope and faith in God. The atmosphere at these gatherings was sombre but mellow because of the soft Bengali lyrics playing in the background. Some were love songs, others stirring national songs, but the mood was getting intense.

At one of these parties, one of the Bengali guests suddenly burst out angrily, 'You have treated us like an inferior race, neglecting us and reducing us to poverty! We will no longer stand for this nonsense!' And thus expostulating, he marched out of the room, leaving the gathering stunned. Until then they were not fully aware of the extent of the animosity simmering amongst them.

The situation progressively worsened and the random skirmishes developed into vicious killings. Tempers were high and disgruntled elements began organising themselves into groups. Very soon these events precipitated into violent genocide that spread fast like an epidemic. Hate and panic were in the air.

Then, before they knew it, war erupted. One day a group of men from the extremist Mukti Bahini attacked Jamshed's house in the middle of the night. The terrified couple crouched under their beds as volleys of gunshots were fired again and again from outside. Luckily none of the bullets entered the house though they pierced the outer walls leaving gaping holes. Gradually the firing stopped and the attackers left. It was a warning for them to run or be killed. They thanked God they were alive.

In this hour of trial, Ziaullah, a Bengali colleague of Jamshed's, came to their aid. In the darkness of night he smuggled them to his house and hid them in the attic, all at the risk of his own life. Bibijan was totally distraught and remained in a constant state of jitters. Jamshed kept his nerve, knowing that remaining calm would be the only way to survive these traumatic times. They were restless and fearful. Food and necessary articles were smuggled in by their friend. Bibijan cooked the bare minimum for food was scarce.

One day they ran out of matches and there was no food. They had to go hungry the whole day. Against his better judgement Jamshed ventured out, though Bibijan had begged him not to. And then it happened with the alacrity of a whiplash! Mukti Bahini had been patrolling the streets all night long. One of them spotted him as he appeared in the darkness and called out imperiously, 'Oye there! Where are you going? Stop!' Jamshed did not stop.

The soldier, seeing him disappear into one of the houses, banged at the door. The banging roused a servant from his sleep and with disheveled clothes and tousled hair, he rushed to open the door. 'Are you hiding traitors in your house?' roared the man. 'There is no one here sir,' stammered the man, 'My master is away on business.'

'Search the house!' shouted the man. The men ransacked the house but found nobody. It was a stroke of good fortune that they did not see the secret entrance to the attic. 'This man is lying!' he shouted to his subordinate who held a rifle. 'Shoot him!' The servant was shot in the head while they shouted, 'You dog! You traitor!' The servant crumpled and fell dead on the floor while blood pooled around him. The men marched out of the house, with a shout, 'Allah-o-Akbar!' and continued their patrol in the unlit deserted streets.

Jamshed and Bibijan, terrified, held their breath as they heard the gunshots below. Jamshed put his hand on his wife's mouth to muffle her scream. Paralysed with fear, they cowered in the dark not daring to light a candle. All night they could hear boots marching in unison but they remained still, not daring to move. They did not sleep a wink that night.

In the following weeks the situation in the land went from bad to worse. They heard of people being pulled out of their houses and being shot by a firing squad. Casualties on both sides soared and the monster of vendetta took hold. The Mukti Bahini lit fires of communalism. West Pakistani soldiers strove ruthlessly to quell the rebellion. Hatred singed every human bond. Friends now became enemies, and both the high and low in society were equally dehumanised. The contagion of violence bulldozed whole communities. The fabric of society was being fractured like shards of glass. The situation was spiraling out of control with the speed of lightning.

As the days wore on hostility magnified between Bengalis and Pakistani troops. People who were thought to be complicit with the opposing group were exterminated. The number of dead multiplied by the day and mass burials became the norm.

Ziaullah could no longer guarantee the safety of the family he was sheltering. Then good news came that special planes were being chartered to repatriate the residents of West Pakistan. With the help of his influential contacts he made plans to get his friend and his wife on one of the first planes that were leaving.

Jamshed, tears in his eyes, profusely thanked his host for saving their lives. 'I shall forever remain in debt to you, I am sorry I cannot ever repay you.' Ziaullah embraced his friend and bid him farewell. 'Don't mention it, my friend. This might have been the best thing I ever did in my life.' Their parting was emotional and tinged with intense relief after the harrowing experience of the preceding weeks.

Numb with fatigue, the couple breathed a sigh of relief as they boarded the plane. As they flew through the blue skies, Bibijan whispered to her husband, ‘My dear, a strange thing has happened. I value my life and yours now more than ever. It is as if we are reborn. I vouch from my heart I will never be afraid again. I have thrown fear out of the window. These horrifying days have taught me to kill fear before it finds a resting place in my heart.’ Jamshed managed a wry smile and squeezed his wife’s hands. He could see that his wife had finally come out of her cocoon.

But in that moment he was reluctant to tell her how his own fears were growing on him, and he wondered if he would ever be completely free of the ghosts of the past few months.

THE FORBIDDEN FRUIT

Sonia had tasted the ripe, lusciously sweet, but forbidden fruit. A tremor shook her body. The man stood before her, strong and masculine, flexing his well-developed muscles and holding her tightly in his arms, murmuring, 'My dearest, I love you.' Her heart had melted like soft snowflakes. She was seized by a virulent passion, intense and powerful, and she surrendered to it. It struck her forcefully, like a landslide that flattened her.

Five years ago, Sonia was married to the man of her dreams who was gentle, loving and graciously caring. He doted on her, devoutly and passionately. Both belonged to a stock of orthodox Christians who were the product of mixed marriages between Hindus and Muslims. They were naturally hybrid but held on to Christian values. The couple had one child who was the apple of their eye, and they nurtured him lovingly. Amongst their friends and family the couple was considered to be born under a lucky star, exemplary in their devotion to each other.

Life was going well for the couple when suddenly everything seemed to be jinxed. One fateful day, when Sonia was out performing household errands, she spotted the man. He was not a stranger for he was an old inhabitant of the area. Oftentimes she had seen her husband engaged in leisurely conversation with him on the street where they crossed each other in the same neighbourhood. He was a tailor by profession and visited people's homes to take orders for stitching clothes. It was a home delivery service, collecting fabric and then delivering the stitched garments. Otherwise his family kept to themselves and his wife was never seen in public.

Then there was a wedding in the family that was announced suddenly. Sonia rummaged through her wardrobe and realised she urgently needed new clothes. She sent for the tailor. He came immediately as if he had been waiting for her call. She would have been more circumspect had she known he had been waiting for this moment. When he appeared at her house he looked more handsome than he did from afar. He had a small French beard and wore a crisp, white *shalwar kameez*. She was alone in the house. He measured her contours to customise the dress. He lingered over every contour. As he did so, each part he touched melted like volcanic lava. He sensed her longing, he lingered and they made love. Once it was over, he left hurriedly like a man escaping his own shame. On her part, she set the guilt aside temporarily.

When her husband came home, gushing over her as usual, she looked normal, calm and composed. Throughout the evening she was silent, stifling emotions in the midst of a virulent turmoil. Her husband was unusually loquacious that evening, perhaps to compensate for her silence. He was a trusting man who loved her wholeheartedly. Her response to him was cold. A distance had already begun to settle between them, like ice on cold surfaces.

The man who was not her husband had greater claims on her now, though he came to the house when the husband was not in. His visits were infrequent, so as not to evoke suspicion, and they had a purpose - to tailor her clothes. With the passage of time he became a familiar figure, both for Sonia's husband and for her young boy who took him for granted without questioning. The unspoken truth had finally dawned on the husband, yet it remained a sacred vow of secrecy, unarticulated, lest it became a reality for him. The husband wrestled with his turmoil in silence. His grief was hidden as exposure would spoil everything. He feigned ignorance, for if he didn't, his reaction, however subdued, could put an end to the marriage. He knew he couldn't live without her. He measured his choices and knew he didn't have any. She suspected he knew and used it to test his love for her. Her faith in him was absolute, she knew he could not fail the biggest trial of their marriage.

The man who had stirred tumult in calm waters, the common tailor, continued to stand at a distance. A storm had brewed between his wife and himself, which he had won, being the man of the house. The wife was in hysterics and he denied all allegations. He could not bear to have his name tarnished, which would violate his Muslim values. He could live a life in sin but could not bear the shame of being stripped naked. He donned his white cap, wore a beard and clothed himself in pristine white attire. Nobody dared to confront him, his strength was in being a man which gave him the license. His wife, duty-bound, surrendered to her fate.

Then a lifetime opportunity blossomed for the husband. He managed to get a job in Canada. This was his great escape. He could salvage his marriage now. Amidst tears and lamentations from a distraught Sonia, he finally managed to persuade her to come with him. He convinced her they would be better off financially. It would be a godsend opportunity for their son to acquire a good education.

A year went by, Sonia and her family had settled in the new land. They assimilated into their new milieu and were content. Her husband continued to love her with undiminished intensity and their bond became stronger. The good old days had returned when the two doted on each other and were the envy of many.

Then one day there was an urgent telephone call. It was the tailor's wife and her voice sounded agonised. She came straight to the point. 'Hanif, my husband, is dying. His last wish is to see you before he goes. It is his death wish.' The call ended abruptly.

Sonia's husband knew it was futile to stop her. She prepared for the journey, said goodbye to her son. When she arrived a day later, he was waiting for her…to die. The family left them alone in the room. They embraced, holding each other tightly. He said hoarsely, 'I am dying, pray for my soul and yours. I could not have had it otherwise.' She wept as if her heart would break. And then he breathed deeply and took his last breath.

She rose and slipped quietly out of the house. Her mind was in turmoil, wondering whether it was the end or beginning of her life. She took a flight back home the same day. She couldn't bear this city anymore, it had too many ghosts and skeletons. The city was virtually dead in its great desolation.

To the end of her days, Sonia remained a devout Christian and a devoted wife. Yet a great lie remained shrouded in her bosom. It was a glaring indictment of herself, where a murky line, between virtue and sin, loyalty and betrayal, stood like a stalled reckoning.

THE FUMES OF WAR

Two women sat in the living room, engaged in an animated discussion that touched a variety of topics including poetry, philosophy and the arts. Their immersion was complete, soul satisfying and profound. The conversation was intercepted by the informal entry of the man of the house, who walked into the room dressed in a grey tweed coat and matching trousers. One of the women, who was a guest but no stranger to him, greeted him cordially. He responded effusively, eager to join the conversation. He loved to talk and was known for his garrulity. Almost instantly he jumped into the conversation, veering it towards his favourite topic - politics. The women graciously opened the space to enable him to voice his opinions. He was an opinionated man who quickly took control of the discourse. Currently war clouds were looming on the horizon and the town was abuzz with dramatic news feeds flashing in the media. The man spoke vociferously on the latest developments. A war veteran, he was convinced that this was his domain and he was best equipped to elaborate on it. The recent capture of two enemy aircraft was the hot topic of the day. He boasted interminably about the superior capability of the army and the air force. He bragged, 'Our army is the best army in the world, nobody can beat us. We might be a beleaguered country, with a bankrupt economy and corrupt political and judicial systems, but you can't deny the moral fibre of our military.' He puffed up his chest, in a self-congratulatory manner.

The woman who was a guest intervened. 'The army has ruled this country for many years and they have to share some of the blame. They are culpable of toppling elected governments and of taking over the reins of governance. We need democracy here to function, not military dictatorships. The army performs best on the battlefield.'

The man looked appalled at this statement, banged his fist on the table and cried excitedly, 'The army intervenes at the behest of civilians. In this country democracy is a sham, the people need to be ruled with an iron hand which is the only way! There is no other way!'

The guest kept her composure and calmly replied, 'Well I for one do not want war, at least not while I'm here. I'm visiting from America. My home is there, my children are there and I want to go back safe and sound. I don't want to die in this country! There appears to be a kind of lockdown and airports are closed. I am very concerned I might be stuck here.'

The man lost his composure and spoke animatedly. 'You do not want to die in this country, where you were born and raised! This is the country for which your parents struggled and gave their lives for freedom from colonisers! You have turned traitor to this country. Why, dying in one's country, and dying for it, is a sacred honour for *me*, and for *any* decent citizen!'

A hush descended on the room and the two women were silenced with no choice but to listen to the man venting his opinions, unaware of their sensibilities.

The man paced the room with his hands waving theatrically in the air. His agitation swelled up, 'You women are anglicised, cocooned in a fantasy world! You live removed from the real world and its harsh reality. This is not poetry! This is war! You who were mentored by nuns in the convent have no idea of the world of men, their deeds of valour and their struggle in wartime. You women live on your little islands and will die on them without exposure to the real world.' The women stared at the man, too stunned to speak, as he continued his monologue.

After this outburst silence hung in the air that further emboldened the man. It ignited him and he continued to harangue his audience. The women listened politely and patiently and dared not disagree.

The women were not distraught. They understood the situation better than he did, and in this way were more in control. Their vision transcended beyond the obvious, their silence was their strength and not an indication of weakness. They could see both sides of the picture. Black and white situations existed only for men like him for whom there were no grey areas and nothing beyond the tangible.

Then abruptly the woman who was his wife decided they had had enough. She took over the reins and confronted him, 'We have heard enough and we beg to disagree. But we do not believe in bullying you into listening to us. Your monologue is full of sound and fury, coming from your military background. We know there will be no war. We cannot afford a war, we are nuclear states, and the rest is braggadocio. This is the empty rhetoric of two states challenging each other and exaggerating their strengths. War is no longer fought by men but by machines. The men who pull the trigger are exterminators, not heroes. They are cowards who wallow in heroism and bravado and violate the dignity of decent, ordinary men.'

The woman, his wife, after venting her feelings sat down defiantly and stoically. The man was stunned. He opened his mouth, thought the better of it and sealed his lips. Suddenly the air in the room cleared, his furrowed brow cleared, the tension in the room diffused and the mood changed. Tea was brought in and the topic was changed. The three chattered amicably. Heated discussions were a norm in this house. They were never taken seriously and soon forgiven. The man, unconcernedly and with gusto, continued to help himself to savoury cookies.

THE LONE WARRIOR

Koel was an elegant woman who exuded a positive energy and purpose in everything she did. She was a successful lawyer, known to champion the cause of the marginalised, especially taking on cases of women's rights and domestic abuse issues. She was a rare woman who lived her life on her own terms, with grace and dignity, and was guided by her personal and professional values of equality and justice. She was fortunate that she had her husband's unwavering support and encouragement to pursue her goals. He was a calm and self-assured man, not one to be easily ruffled. He celebrated her success and stood behind her when she faced challenges to her cause, bolstering her resolve to continue and never to renounce the path she had chosen.

Koel came home one day and announced with quiet satisfaction that the legislation for equal pay for women in the workplace had been passed. 'I worked for it day and night, and today it happened. It was an uphill task; men, and many women too, opposed it.' Her husband rose from his reclining sofa to applaud her. 'This legislation will go a long way in clearing roadblocks for gender equality,' she said fervently, her voice breaking with emotion.

Koel's expertise in law was well known but very few understood the passion and struggle behind it. As a child she had witnessed her father's arrest, imprisonment and ultimately death by hanging for a crime he did not commit. The perpetrators were powerful men who were able to bend the law to their will. The family had suffered long and hard as a result. This experience, heartbreaking as it was, was her strongest motivation to enter the legal profession and dedicate her life to ensuring that the law delivered justice to everyone.

As a lawyer she had to push hard to make change happen, there were too many roadblocks built by the rich and powerful. To her utter astonishment she was often thwarted by the very women whose battles she fought. It dawned on her that women were not yet ready to be liberated and that they embraced the very chains that shackled them. They were content to stand behind their men, conditioned through the generations to accept their subservient role. This lone warrior repeatedly faced deep-seated contempt from women who not only accepted their status quo, but vigorously resisted any attempt to change it. She found blistering bias, hate and cruelty erupting from their wombs. No woman escaped the wrath of her sisterhood. As for the men, they were not going to easily relinquish their princely kingdom, offering sometimes just condescension or lip service.

Koel knew it was not easy to change this mind-set. Women mocked her and pulled her down, pouring blistering invective and abusive scorn on her person. When their virulent tongues scarred her, she refused to let their poison taint her. The voices of these angry women grew louder. 'She is breaking our societal norms! Traitor! She will destroy the family hearth. She will kill our babies in the womb.' The ranting went on and on as Koel battled against anti-abortion laws and gender equality at work. She stirred up a controversial storm when antagonists spewed vitriol viciously. Only one man stood by her - her husband! He was her staunchest supporter even though he was not one of the stakeholders!

Koel had a vision. She saw light at the end of the tunnel and pursued it single-mindedly. The stakes were high and she could not retreat. Failure at this point was not an option - it was everything or nothing. She did not have the comfort of withdrawal, fear or surrender. She was already too far out at sea, an intrepid sailor, to pause midway. She steeled her spine and fought back.

And then a tragic incident happened in a remote village. A middle-aged woman was gang-raped by five men. They stripped her naked and made her walk in the streets, whilst men, older and younger, pelted stones at her. When night fell, the woman walked in excruciating pain to her house. The doors were shut on her. Her husband shouted, 'Don't ever enter my house. You will never see your children again. You have shamed us all!' That night the woman sheltered at a friend's house. The friend's husband had abandoned her and their three children and married another woman. She had wanted to file for divorce but nobody in the village was willing to help her. Then a woman from an NGO had introduced the friend to Koel who took up her case and won.

The friend thought that Koel would be able to help the woman as well and the next day the two women took a bus to the city and headed for Koel's office. This incident was followed by an uproar. NGOs spurred the outrage and the story went viral. Koel took up the case, the culprits were arrested and convicted. Koel's name was splashed on the headlines of the major newspapers. This was a rude awakening for the public. The denigration of women, the inhumanity of it all, was a blemish on the national psyche. The public cried for change and all the TV channels supported them. The mood of the public was shifting like a tsunami.

The country was changing and Koel had made headlines. Triumphant with her success she pushed further. She fought harder for women in the workplace, for their safety and sense of dignity. Now women who had long suffered domestic abuse saw her as a beacon of hope. They knew that this invincible woman would stand with them and fight for their rights and their worst fears dissolved. Many stood firmly with her.

Koel managed to give hope to poor women who had been abused by their families, husbands and in-laws and changed their self-image. She had changed the face of society. But she had, unwittingly, committed the grave error of reaching too far. Society was not yet ready for it. There was controversy and voices from opposing forces grew louder and more bellicose.

And then one of the women from the fraternity of lawyers, motivated by professional jealousy, stood up against Koel, charging her with subverting abortion laws which she said had led to waves of abortions. There was an incident of a woman dying at an abortion clinic. This was sensationalised by the media, whipping up a frenzied reaction to all the work that had been done. Subsequent to this incident, many women from the legal fraternity echoed the condemnation, triggering a movement against Koel to force her to give up her practice. She was shattered and outraged. Her husband urged her to remain strong. Her supporters came forward and took to the streets with chants of 'Stay firm, Koel, stay firm! Save us!'

Then the inevitable happened. It was a day like any other when Koel announced to her husband that she had to tell him something urgently. 'I know you will be shocked and grieved but I have decided to call it a day! I have decided to quit.'

Her husband was stunned! 'Why now Koel, when you are almost there?'

She answered flatly, 'I can't take it, anymore! I have been on the stormy seas for too long and am exhausted to my bones. I have considered it through and I know that time is crucial. What I have accomplished is enough for this moment in time. If women are against abortion laws, then I do not want to deliver a foetus instead of a full-term baby. But one thing is clear to me, whatever I have accomplished up until now will, at some point, change the face of society. It is the beginning and it is my firm belief that many stalwarts will come in the days ahead and will carry it forward. The wheels of time do not remain static, they will continue moving, higher and higher. As for me, I know my time has come. I do not grieve or regret.'

Her husband shook his head incredulously and took her into his arms, 'Well, I call it the end of an era that ends not with a whimper, but with a big bang.' She laughed, musing over the generosity of her husband who never ceased to surprise her.

THE MAN IN THE PINK SHIRT

It was the stark pink shirt and the blue tie on the young man that caught Sarosh's attention on that sultry afternoon at Cafe Beach. The man lounged in his chair across the room, his narrow unblinking eyes fixed on her face. Initially when she became aware of his scrutiny she struggled to avert her eyes, and then intermittently her eyes rested on him. His look was pointed, conspiratorial, throwing her into confusion. Momentarily she was flattered that she had caught the attention of a man, but now she was in no mood for coquetry. Sarosh was a mature older woman in the winter of her life, circumspect of strangers. Moreover, she was in the company of her formidable elder sister and suave sister-in-law in whose shadows she had lived. They kept up a convivial chatter, diving avidly in and out of topics.

The cafe was bustling with people flocking in for a bite in the middle of a sultry afternoon. The continuous flow did not interrupt or divert the man sitting across the room with a fixed sneer on his face. He was accompanied by a woman and man who conversed in hushed tones. The woman was young and pretty with flaming red hair, attired in formal office dress. She sat upright with her back to Sarosh, smoking a cigarette. The other man, seated on the third chair, stood out in a red shirt and yellow tie. Other than his flamboyant attire, he sat passively. All three sat in joint camaraderie, wrapped in conversation, isolated from the world around, except for one - the man in the pink shirt.

'Excuse me!' said the young man, rising abruptly and coming to

Sarosh's table. 'Have I seen you before? You look very familiar.' He was facing Sarosh, his muscular arms clenched tightly on the table. For a moment the three women were stunned, taken aback by his bluntness, something they were not accustomed to.

Sarosh replied emphatically, 'No, no! I have never seen you before, young man. It's a mistake!'

'You are lying, lady, you know this is not our first meeting,' he replied more assertively than before, leaning over the table.

At this point, Sarosh's sister recovered her composure and rose quietly and said, 'Excuse me, I am going to the restroom,' and cautiously edged past the man who was blocking her space. The third woman, the sister-in-law, partly assessing the situation and partly not, rummaged in her bag for her mobile phone and began texting furiously, feigning a calmness she was far from feeling. Meanwhile Sarosh remained rooted to her spot. Time ticked slowly. The air was full of suspense.

'I clearly remember the last time I set eyes on you, my lady. You were not alone, you were accompanied by a man, apparently your close associate. You had a disagreement with him, a squabble that turned into a fight, and then you sought refuge in our den. Your man was drinking heavily and lost control. He could have harmed you. *Do you remember now*?' He glowered as he brought his face close to her. 'The police were on the watch for him that night and could have arrested you both. I saved you, and now you have the audacity to look me in the face and pretend that you do not know me - I, your saviour!' He banged his fist on the table.

Sarosh was stupefied. She shrank from him, her spine tingling. A flood of memories came racing back and she was paralysed with fear. She had cast that episode from her mind long ago and now it came back to haunt her. She trembled at the thought of him turning predator. He was part of a gang of armed men who stalked the streets at night to loot unwary passersby. Only a criminal could catch a criminal. She had known that fateful day that she was in jeopardy and that they were on the hunt for prey. That night they played Robin Hood and had saved her life.

Now the man, whose name she did not recall, stood challenging her, swaying his muscular body like a boxer. She noticed his cheap attire, his flimsy polyester pants and his dusty black shoes. Glancing over his shoulder, she looked at his companions, pretending not to notice the scene being created by their friend. They remained in the shadows.

Sarosh was at her wits end till she saw her sister walking back to their table accompanied by another man who was apparently the manager of the cafe. She breathed a sigh of relief. The manager casually stopped at customers tables to enquire solicitously of their needs. Then he came to Sarosh's table and politely asked, 'Ladies, did you like our food and service. Do you need anything else?'

He ignored the other man at the table, as if he was invisible. The ladies replied graciously, they were happy with the quality of the food and service. Sarosh, wanting to ease tension, said enthusiastically, 'The food was delicious, just to my liking. We shall visit again soon, Sir.' With a sideways glance, Sarosh noticed the young man turned red and shifted uncomfortably, his braggadocio vanishing, and with head lowered, he quickly slipped away. Slick man, thought Sarosh. He walked up to his companions, whispered something after which they rose and walked hurriedly to the exit.

The three women thanked the manager profusely for rescuing them from an ugly situation. He warned them, 'In future be wary of such men, they like nothing better than to trap decent women like you.' They thanked him again, collected their bags, and left. Sarosh was quiet, her downcast face lowered, her mind in turmoil, grateful that tonight's episode had not hurt her in any way.

THE MIGRANT

The man walked briskly on the busy street with his head bent low, oblivious to his surroundings. A short, bald man in khaki shorts, who was walking at a distance behind, recognised him, quickened his pace, and called out loudly, 'Hey Roomi, my brother, stop, stop!' The man continued to walk on at his steady pace without looking back. The bald man finally caught up and slapped him on the back, crying breathlessly, 'Hey! Have you gone deaf and dumb, my brother? I've been calling out to you, but you refuse to hear.'

The man turned, collected himself, smiled and said, 'Excuse my absent-mindedness, my friend. I didn't hear you. And what a surprise! I did not expect to see you here, of all the places,' he added, gently pulling away his arm.

The bald man, in a state of excitement, having met his friend from old, rambled on, 'You remember when we last met, we were back home, both escaping from the enemy. Bombs were falling all around us, and that day we thought we would die. After that we lost each other in the chaos of the war. It is a miracle we survived it, and now here we are in this strange land that is destined to be our host country. Just think of it, we have both ended up in the same country.'

The other man, tall and lean, with a long face and set jaw, who was given to brooding, said sadly, 'Destiny has strange ways of leading us to unknown paths. I could never have thought in my wildest dreams that I would land here, in this otherwise glittering city of romance and glamour, but which is cold and alien to me.' He looked around at the sea of faces surrounding them, dressed in bright, chic clothes, some walking hand in hand, and chattering gaily. They were an enigmatic people, keeping a distance from those from foreign lands. They were circumspect, with a hint of veiled hostility. They were privileged, untouched by suffering and trauma, living their lives in a state of amnesia, each one cosseted in their comfort zones.

'Where are you heading? If you have nothing in particular on your mind today, why don't we go to some place for coffee? I know a very nice place nearby,' the bald man offered. 'We can catch up with each other in a lighter mood over a hot drink.'

The man who was given to brooding replied, 'Good idea, we can talk with leisure inside, I need to know how you are faring.'

The two men entered a quaint coffee shop, with small, tightly squeezed in tables, and big colourful posters on the walls. A picture of a pretty model showing off her orange dress with outstretched, bare arms looked down at them, a hint of coquetry in her eyes. Soft non-intrusive music filled the room, soothing their spirits. A cordial waitress, with a freshly starched white apron, led them to a small table for two. 'Good day, gentlemen, what can I serve you?' she asked, smiling. She was a pretty girl, holding herself gracefully.

The bald man ordered a pastry and coffee. The other man said, 'One coffee please, with no milk and no sugar.' Then he stretched his legs and sighed, a deep sigh that shook his body.

The bald man rambled on, ‘I can’t wait to tell you my story. It is a long narrative, mind you, and not one without pain and tribulation. When I came to this country, I was a desperate man. I landed at night, in a boat of migrants, crowded with men, women and children. Mercifully we were not deported. Months passed and I was living in makeshift shelters, penniless and going hungry for days. I was beside myself, fearing that I might never make it and be forced to return. Finally I got acquainted with some people who guided me on how to get employment. Now, after two years, I am employed in a construction company with a decent salary. Back home, my father had also worked as a contractor for a company and I assisted him. By the way, he died in the war. My mother had already been dead for some years. My wife and two kids have joined me here and things are finally moving ahead.’ He sat back with a sigh of relief. ‘Oh my God! There I go rambling on, and you have not spoken a word up until now. It is your turn now to tell your story.’

The man, who was given to brooding, paused before he spoke softly, ‘My story is very different from yours. Back home, as you know, I came from a distinguished family, people who took their entitlement for granted, living a soft and easy life. Then the war started and the state crumbled. Our only concern was our safety as blizzards of bombs pelted down on us. My parents died in the war, a month after the heavy bombings started. My father had refused to evacuate when they started bombing the city. He was a proud and stubborn man, and I remember his words, “I shall not leave my beloved city, they can bomb it down to ashes." My mother went along with whatever he did. They died together when the house crumbled. Three days later, my brother and I were rescued from the debris. It was a miracle that we were alive, intact in body and spirit, and delivered with a second life. Afterwards we went hungry for days, living in makeshift shelters through which the sun slanted in on hot days and rain pelted through cracks. Months later my brother disappeared and to this day I know nothing of his whereabouts. He was a headstrong boy, like my father, and couldn't see himself broken. He escaped more from his own desolation than from a war-ravaged city. Before he ran away he would moan daily in a dull monotonous tone, "There are no survivors in war, only skeletons and dead men. In place of bustling cities, there are silent cemeteries, in place of a vibrant milieu, there are vultures screaming and tearing down on maimed corpses, turning them overnight into untouchables who nobody wants to bury. There are no winners in war, only losers pretending to win." He was a poet, and I knew his heart was broken beyond measure.'

The man's voice lowered, exhausted from so much talking. The bald man, who had been listening intently, said reassuringly, 'Oh, come on man, put all that behind you. I understand you went through a great trauma, and so did I, but we need to put all that behind us. The present we face has its own challenges; embrace it and it will embrace you, reject it, and you will find yourself against a wall.' With that he stroked his broad shoulders, 'See, my shoulders are strong enough to bear my weight, like a heavyweight champion. Practice, my man, practice is the trick of the trade. My father always told me, "Son, life is harsh and never easy, prepare yourself for the worst, and something good will come out of it."'

The brooding man with sharp chiseled features, who had been handsome in his day, shifted his gaze momentarily to the waitress hovering over the tables. He distractedly threw her a quick smile, and then continued in a low tone, 'I have struggled to find a job here that suits my tastes, but it has turned out to be a futile task. Recently I was hired as an apprentice in a publishing house, but they pay a lean salary and I can hardly make ends meet. The apartment where I live is home to rats that scuttle throughout the night and don't let me sleep. My friend, you see I have the weirdest bedfellows. I am a lonely man in the midst of a bustling moving city of millions, a stranger to its many ways. Or, perhaps I am too old to be broken like a wild horse.' Here he paused for a while, and then said with a deep sigh, 'You know, sometimes I feel my soul has aged more than my physical self. I am inhabited by an aging soul.'

The bald man said again with greater urgency, 'Oh, come on man, this country offers many opportunities. Seize the first one that comes your way, even if it lies on the wayside.'

The brooding man who barely heard him continued looking into his empty cup of coffee and uttered solemnly, 'I am like this cup: empty and drained out. The stains bear testimony to the coffee I consumed. A memory hangs in the air of decaying cities and a lost civilization that an entirely new generation alone can rebuild with its fresh blood and sweat.' The man's face was streaked with tears.

The waitress came to clear the table and politely asked, 'Gentlemen, did you enjoy the coffee?'

The brooding man for the first time looked closely at her and was surprised to see her pretty features, her bold carriage and her enticing smile. Somewhere in his mind it struck a chord, he blushed, and was ashamed of his own brokenness. A ray of sunshine, in a flash, entered his heart, uplifting his mood. 'Why, yes we did,' he replied, and added, 'I must come here again, and next time I will eat a hearty meal.'

When he left the waitress, to her surprise, saw a handful of notes lying beneath the bill. She smiled and paused for a while, 'Nice man,' she murmured, and moved on to the next in the queue of waiting customers.

When the two friends embraced, they promised to meet soon again. Yet, the roads they had taken ran parallel and had no nexus or meeting point. Perhaps, later at some other crossroad, they would run into each other again and do a little 'catching up'. Or one of the two men might simply be swallowed up in the dense sea of human faces, and later be thrown up offshore, like a dead fish, by a tumultuous wave. People walking on the shore that day would comment, 'This handsome guy was not a good swimmer, and somehow carved his own destiny.' Or the same man might, one day, discover a survival instinct in himself, and keep up the strife long enough to reach his destination.

THE MINION

A crowd of people had gathered at the auditorium to attend a literary festival that had lately been the buzz of the town. Intellectuals, literary men and women had flocked on a weekend to hear their favourite writers. As they waited for the doors to open they exchanged small talk, enquired about each other's intellectual and social pursuits. At the same time they seized on the opportunity to connect with the celebrities, a medley of writers, poets and journalists.

Finally, the doors opened and people entered the hall. The moderator, a mousy looking woman with nondescript features but a chic hairdo that pumped style into an otherwise plain looking face, came to the podium. She had a no-nonsense approach and, in a brusque manner, set guidelines for the speakers and audience.

There was some confusion at the door as some latecomers searched for empty seats. The hall had been booked beyond capacity. Some harsh words were exchanged before people were accommodated. The moderator looked disturbed and called out sternly, 'Calm down! Take your seats! We are ready to begin.' Suddenly the voices stopped, silence fell and the crowd quickly settled down.

The moderator introduced the speakers who were all stars in a literary galaxy. The books of these writers had been published recently and were available outside the hall. The first speaker talked eloquently and philosophically, 'In the process of writing, a writer opens a window into his subliminal world and has a definitive voice and worldview. I found my voice after much practice. This is the core of my writing. My readers know me through my voice. This is the way I connect with them.' Then he went on to talk at length about his book, a memoir, and his source of inspiration. The audience soaked up all that was said.

An elderly man sitting in the front row was deeply immersed in the talk. He was of slight build, half bald and had a slight stoop. He was one of them, belonging to the fraternity of poets and writers, consigned now to the role of listener rather than speaker. He had been sidelined at this event; his creativity had diminished in recent years since he had not written or published any books.

A man sitting next to him recognised him and cried in surprise, 'Hey, aren't you the writer Asif Zakariya? You were the speaker at my commencement when I graduated five years ago.'

The man so addressed shuffled in his seat. 'I am indeed Zakariya, the years have caught up quickly. Yes, I remember that commencement, your principal was kind enough to invite me.'

The other man said, 'You know, your speech that day was so motivational, it changed my life. You told us that each individual was born for a purpose, to find the meaning of his life and to pursue it. I pursued my passion, was committed and have recently completed my first book.'

A flicker of joy lit up the Zakariya's eyes, 'You must have had it in you and that is why you made it. Anyway, I'm happy I was instrumental in facilitating you. It doesn't happen every day. A candle, if hollow, will not burn.'

At this point, a lady sitting on the other side of them, whispered irritably, 'Shhh! Can't you sit quietly and listen? Why did you come here then? Was it to disturb our peace?'

The two men were embarrassed and kept silent.

When the event ended, the crowd began to disperse. Zakariya, never in a rush to go anywhere, rose slowly. The other man followed close behind, vying for his attention. 'Would you do me the favour of joining me for a cup of coffee, Sir?'

Zakariya nodded, 'I would love to. Any place of your choice.' He did not venture an opinion himself as he was unfamiliar with such places that were mostly favoured by younger people. They entered a small coffee shop that radiated coziness and warmth. Zakariya looked satisfied and settled for a secluded corner. 'I like small spaces for their peace and quiet, an escape from a rowdy crowd.' He lit a cigarette and drew a long puff. The younger man sat expectantly with his hands in his lap. Zakariya scrutinised him closely and liked what he saw. The man had an ear to listen, enough humility to learn and an openness to enter untraveled and unknown spaces.

'Do you mind, Sir, if I ask you a question?' the younger man asked earnestly.

Zakariya replied kindly, 'You are welcome.'

The younger man paused, swallowed and then spoke again, 'Why Sir, why were you not on the stage tonight? You are a greater luminary than that bunch over there.'

'Well, yours is not an extraordinary question and neither is my answer. Every dog has his day, and I have had mine. It doesn't take long to morph from a celebrity to a has-been. Fame is fickle. But then remember, life is not only about accolades, it is the arduous journey of a man finding his singular self, and when we near our goal, we seek nothing else.'

'Are you sure there isn't anything else that you are not telling me?'

Zakariya gave a start, choked over his hot coffee, steadied himself, and started to narrate his story. He was an otherwise reserved man, averse to talking about himself. But perhaps it is sometimes easier to open one's heart to a stranger rather than an intimate friend or relative. Strangers might be less judgmental and more empathetic. Intimate relationships were complex, carried too much baggage. For a long time he had desperately needed to purge himself and unburden his great load.

'You are a shrewd man and I won't disappoint you today. Now listen very carefully. I was in the prime of my life and my career was at its height. I had published many books and believe me they were a success. I was one of those fortunate writers with both money and fame. To crown it all, I was in love with a beautiful woman who was my inspiration. We had married despite the disapproval of our families. Breaking many familial bonds, we tied the conjugal knot. I have never known greater bliss. We rarely disagreed or wrangled. Everything was going fine and we were planning a baby, or at least I was. She was evasive on this issue. Then one day my half-brother came to live with us. He was a disrespectful man, but I couldn't turn him out. He stayed at home all day, lounging around, whilst I went to work. If I had only known the mischief he would brew in my house, I would have turned him out long ago.

'One day, my wife came to me, clasped my hands, and said in a hushed voice, "I have something to tell you. Promise you will forgive me. I will die if you don't." I could feel my heart sinking, as a bell of premonition rang. She continued quietly with her eyes burning, "I'm leaving you. I cannot live with you any longer."

I listened to her, my mind in complete turmoil, as I weighed a million conjectures. After what seemed an eternity, I asked her, "Just give me one good reason and then you can go. I will not hold you a minute longer."

Dry-eyed and matter-of-factly she answered, "I am in love with your half-brother."

'"Have you gone crazy?" I screamed, losing control. The image of my half-brother, slovenly and sly, rushed to my mind, and I shuddered. "He has beguiled you, that scoundrel, and you have fallen into his trap. Shame on you! You will live to regret this!"

'Momentarily, she looked crestfallen, but then holding her head up and looking straight into my eyes, she said, "All is fair in love and war."

'With those words something broke inside me. I looked at her incredulously, and was ashamed, more for myself than her. How could someone whom I had loved with such passion do this?'

Zakariya lowered his head as the young man looked on. 'From that moment I ceased to believe in anything. How could this happen to me, who had written stories about the lives of others, created full-flesh characters, handled complex issues. I considered myself shrewd, trusted my own judgement. I felt a complete fool, a loser. I knew at that moment that nothing in life was permanent, least of all our most cherished relationships. In a nutshell, my life up until now had been a mockery, a façade, and I was the imposter who now shunned his own face in the mirror. From that day onwards, my creativity dried up and I never wrote a word again.'

The younger man was at a loss for words, like having to offer condolences to a bereaved man, beyond words or human sympathy. There was a long, uninterrupted silence between them. Outside, night had fallen, there was a lull in the air, heavy, grim and brooding. It was time to take leave. As they parted outside, the older man squeezed his hand. 'Thank you for listening to my story. You have helped to purge a wound from my mind. For years I had locked my grief in my heart, more from shame, and was tortured no end. Tonight, after many years, you helped me to relieve that burden. I shall sleep soundly today.' Here he paused, and when he spoke again his voice was low and guttural. 'Mark my words, young man, whether you are in a relationship or not, I don't know, but always remember that the illusion of love is the only reality we will ever know. The candle of love that we light will flicker in the wind but we must learn to hold strong.'

THE OLD TYPEWRITER

'That is the only piece I have left now,' declared the elderly salesman, rubbing his hands. 'You will never regret having it.' I clearly remember the day I bought my Remington. And now here it rests in my small study - a priceless relic from old times. It has proved to be as sturdy as the elderly salesman had promised so many years ago, though now it is somewhat discoloured. The ravages of time and the sufferings of overuse have resulted in its black paint peeling off in places and its keyboard dimmed and almost indistinct. Dust and rust have slowly crept into its crevices, giving it an antique look and a peculiar character. No longer in use, it is still an essential part of me, interlocked into my being like a vital organ. As I gently touch the keys I cannot fight back a wave of nostalgia that overcomes me like a black cloud.

The Remington has been my ally through thick and thin. It has filled the spaces in my heart that were voids of loneliness - some deeper than others. It has held me together when my relationships were precarious and on the verge of breaking up, when the pressures of working life rocked my peace of mind, and also when my beautiful wife Sarah abandoned me. She said that she found me to be cold and detached and accused me of neglect. She said that I had failed to reach out to her in the way she desired.

The divorce broke me but I nurtured my grief in solitude. Over the years, when I reflected on my marital life, I realised how demanding Sarah had been. I could not satisfy her, even in the best of times. I wince when I remember her parting words to me, 'Daniyal, the bottom line is that you're an insensitive man. I'm leaving because I know you'll never change, and I am sick and tired of having my heart broken again and again.' Her voice quivering, she continued, 'You know I kept dreaming of the day when you and I could live in blissful togetherness, but I know that day will never come.' I remember her tear-stained face and my bewilderment as if it were yesterday.

I still cannot, and perhaps never will, understand the mystery that is called a woman. I gave Sarah everything - a comfortable home, beautiful children and above all, fidelity, and yet she felt she had nothing. Can any man satisfy a woman's heart? A mere mortal like me doesn't have an answer to that age-old question. She was raised in a single parent home and avoided talking about her growing years, that I had a gut feeling that it had been tough. All she said was, 'My father was always aloof and let me do things my way because he wasn't bothered.' She was one of those restive people whose quest for happiness always consumes them. She said, 'I feel inadequate in so many ways - and most of all as a mother. Parenting doesn't come easy to me. I have no role models in my life.' I knew from the beginning that we were destined to separate as the unhappiness threatened to engulf us both like a forest fire.

By lucky providence the girls remained unaffected. I was devastated but I could not break her heart and of my own volition, gave the custody of the girls to her. I think it worked out well. They have grown up to be well-adjusted beautiful girls, and more importantly they seem unscarred. At the end of the day this is what really matters to me. I really missed having them around me, but I knew that I could never take care of them the way she could. I was kind and indulgent with them, and to my surprise they are my anchor now. They have their mother's beautiful features with her green, sun-washed eyes. I am comforted by the thought that the melancholy look that haunts Sarah's eyes is absent from theirs.

My daughters would visit me once a month and over the years they injected a new life into me. They have pretty names, Sarosh and Marie, and were joyful, responsive and caring. Sarosh, the younger one, would run spontaneously into my arms and give me a bear hug. 'Dad!' she would say and as I embraced her, and she would cling to me, craving affection and not wanting to let go. The elder one, Marie, was a quiet child, and kept a wary distance at first, before she too would jump into my welcoming arms. Their mother would drop them off at my place but would not enter my house. 'Now what are we going to do today?' Marie would ask as soon as her shyness faded.

'Anything you suggest, darling - eating out or the movies?'

The girls relished the pretty gifts I gave them and the Godiva chocolates which I bought for them. 'Dad, we love them!' they would cry, as I would watch them open the carefully wrapped boxes with delicate hands. Sometimes we would go to the cinema and then snack at nearby places, tucking into hamburgers. Or we would drive to the lush green countryside, where we would jog and play games. By the end of the day we would be ready to drop with fatigue.

Then it would be time to take them home and I would drop them at their mother's house which was nestled amongst a long line of modest but practical townhouses. These monthly excursions filled me with calm and I would be like a spirit soothed. Then the clock would start ticking again, waiting for the next four weeks to pass.

Apart from our link through our daughters, my relationship with Sarah was behind me - as much as things could be pushed into the past. I knew I could never make a clean break with the past and blindfold myself to all the heartaches that clung to me. I knew that I now had the space I craved to be with my trusted Remington. Perhaps that was why Sarah had hated it like a dreaded foe. Her mocking words still ring in my years, like jarring music, 'You and your typewriter are one of a kind! I have no patience for either of you!'

My Remington and I had together churned out stories after stories, essays and also research articles. I had an extensive vocabulary picked up from years of reading the classics and this tool helped me immensely. Some of my works were neatly stacked in drawers, never seeing the light of day. Some I sent to magazines and if I was lucky they got published. I was skilled at crafting stories but when it came to getting them printed, I would get the shivers and it was as if I was naked and exposed. But I shunned the limelight and would rather retire into the quiet with my Remington. We were both incorrigibly reclusive.

I was delighted and astonished when one of my novels actually made it big. I had been working on it for five years! I had finally hit the jackpot. It won a literary award. The news splashed headlines. I was on television telling people about it. I remember my first interview when I was asked what had prompted me to write the book, 'Well it is a memoir, as most first books are. The central character, Haroon, turns out to be a reflection of me. He goes on a travel adventure, which becomes a kind of odyssey into his inner self.'

When I was asked whom I owed my life's achievements to, I answered, 'My typewriter, of course.'

The commentator laughed, 'Well, jokes aside Mr Daniyal, will you tell me honestly?'

And my reply was, 'I just told you, my greatest inspiration is my typewriter.' What he never understood and what I could not explain to him, I will tell you, dear reader, this immobile instrument on which my hands played, was my blessed sanctuary. Warm and generous, it urged me to tap my feelings, as I dived into the depths of my mind. No friend could give me that unconditional support, that licence to spell out whatever I needed to say. Here my mind was its own censor, filtering my thoughts and probing the truth.

And then the unexpected happened! I fell in love with Alina, a teacher at a school for disabled children that was in my neighbourhood. One day after a few casual meetings, we ran into each other at our favourite eatery. She was an avid reader like me, and we started off by discussing and dissecting books we had read. We had much in common and she loved the theatre and movies as much as I did.

I was emotionally fragile at this time and unable to cope with my loneliness. Over the years, I had settled into a comfortable niche within myself, and was convinced I could live my life in solitude and would not be able to take the turbulence of marriage. But I had not calculated my craving for company, especially the warmth and feminine touch of a woman. Sitting with Alina in a café one day, drinking coffee, I asked her about her life and was surprised to find her to be quite candid, 'Gosh, it's been ten years since I got divorced. Time flies! I admit it took me quite a while to get over the trauma. We were misfits from the start, he never understood me, and then started the cycle of abuse. In a perverted way, he wanted to possess me wholly, body and soul, and would throw a fit when I tried to break loose from his control. He was deadly jealous of my friends and anyone dear to me. Well, it's over now and I'm relieved. Anyway, since then I have had only myself to rely upon. I value independence. I was never one to be told how I should live my life.'

I listened attentively as she kept talking. 'In retrospect,' she continued, 'I remember my father telling me, "Alina, I know I need not ever worry about you. I am confident you will take care of yourself, in good times and in adversity." My parents are now dead. They were the only two people who ever cared about me. I am entirely on my own. I love my work, and that's it.'

I looked at her in admiration, seeing a woman who is conditioned to look only into the future - a woman who has endured in broken situations. Then I told her my story about my divorce and my children. 'The divorce was inevitable,' I told her, 'She was never satisfied with anything I did, however hard I tried. It was a dead end from the beginning.' Since I was never comfortable talking about my inner conflicts, I quickly switched to my daughters who are the centre of my life and who visit me regularly.

She was watching me closely, 'Your story is strangely similar to mine, except that I don't have children. I know I could never have borne the responsibility of raising a child all on my own. If I can take care of myself, that's enough for me,' she said with a laugh. Ah, that beautiful smile!

I told her I was a writer and devoted to my work. She was impressed. 'I have always admired writers, they are delicate and sensitive people,' she laughed.

I squeezed her hand and embraced her, feeling her warm body and the aroma of her perfume clinging to her body. I was overcome and it struck me that after many years I now missed the feel of a woman. I loved her gaiety and her light banter. I finally found that I was being drawn out of myself.

When we next met, I surprised her with a ring. She cried out with pleasure, as she proudly twirled it on her slender finger. We were in a trance-like mood and things were moving faster than I had imagined.

Later I introduced her to my girls who connected with her shyly, their reserve perhaps meaning that they were a little bit jealous.

Coming back to the present, Alina and I got married yesterday. It happened so quickly that I remained in a state of incredulity, of feeling settled and yet uprooted at the same time. I was like a man who has wandered for years and then suddenly stumbles across a mystical pathway that instantly delights and terrifies him. Or was it like coming home? Whatever this feeling is, I do know that I am happy, like I once was many years ago, and this time around, I'm not going to spoil it.

Now as I stand in front of my Remington, my companion through the ages, I feel we are both in different time periods. The experience of growing up was one threshold I climbed, and the typewriter another one that I crossed in the prime of my life. It is sadly dysfunctional now, replaced by a slick and smart computer, its dynamism absent, but the intimacy remains. Looking at it now, I experience the first glimpse of the ravages of old age, and my own yearning to live beyond a dying relationship. I touch it wistfully, feeling its passive heat, I whisper, 'You were my first love.' Did I hear a groan, or was I imagining it? With a deep sigh, I gingerly lifted it up to take outside. In the garden I went straight to the shed. Picking up an axe and a garden tool resting in a rusted toolbox, I hacked the typewriter to pieces. My mind was numb, conscious only of the killer in me. Before I knew it, the body once called 'Remington', lay in pieces, broken beyond recognition. I took a garbage bag, and put the remains into it, and threw it into the garbage bin.

No trace, no memories! Perhaps all new beginnings are destined to start this way. I have now embarked on my second journey.

THE PRICE OF LOVE

The woman has been living with her married son for some years now. The dynamics between them have shifted subtly but surely. The woman's son is dependent on his wife as they are all living in her house, and is wary of her to say the least. He sees his power waning, and being a fainthearted lad, is not one to assert himself. He gives an inch, she takes a mile, and he finds his space narrowing. Their two children sense all this and take the side of the parent who is in control at the time. The elder child, a daughter, knows her place in the household, and is therefore compliant, whilst the younger child, a son, has not yet picked up the nuances of the situation.

The mother lives in her shell to protect her dignity, oftentimes negotiating her way through what seems like perilous terrain. She tries to please them in small ways. She does not say much, but her son seems to pick up words though not articulated. There is a vicious cycle going on. Her son is given to episodes of anger, and she finds that the less she says, the more he rages. Sometimes his rages invoke terror in her.

The wife is smug about the declining dynamics between the mother and son that she has herself partly instigated, and rewards the husband for his allegiance with special favours, drawing him closer as he distances himself from his mother. There is a push and shove going on. The wife takes her children under her wing and they feel safe and comforted by her love for them. They know that they can now easily distance themselves from their grandmother who has become persona non grata in the family. The nuclear family itself becomes more unified in the process. Seeing a solitary path ahead, the woman has nowhere to go and nothing to hold on to as her life's anchors gradually slip away from her.

Thus, life goes on and the woman's outer shell has by now hardened, and she has become accustomed to the dark drama being played against her. She becomes a shadowy figure, moving silently in the house, walking from room to room, like an interloper, struggling to escape notice. Leaving is not an option as there is nowhere for her to go. She knows the tragic truth that even if she did leave, she would not be missed. So she stays, pretending nothing is amiss. Her son and his family also keep up a pretence of normalcy, having distanced themselves enough to cease any contact with her.

The woman spends most of the day in a nearby park, watching the trees sway in the wind, a medley of wild birds stirring up a cacophony and squirrels hopping tirelessly amidst green grass. She is more comfortable here, being with nature and friendly creatures who do not treat her like a stranger. In these surroundings she finds her solace. She reminiscences about her childhood when her parents pampered her and made much of her as she was the only daughter among three rowdy, rumbustious brothers who teased her mercilessly but loved her fiercely. She was her father's princess who could never do any wrong. Those were days that were idyllically happy and peaceful. She felt a lump in her throat when these memories flooded back.

Then there were the years of adulthood, when she was married to a man who was not of her choice, but who had pursued her and would not give up. He turned out to be quite strange, and their marriage dragged on like a run-down vehicle on a bumpy road, hiccupping from shortage of fuel. He shouted at her constantly, argued and grumbled, more at odds with himself than with her. Yet he blamed her for all his troubles, and she became his punching bag. She was too timid to quit and held on. He changed jobs frequently as his quick temper made it difficult for him to continue in one place for long. They had a son together and they dreamed of raising a fine boy who would be their superhero. But then her husband met with an accident and died quickly, leaving her alone to raise their son. The boy drifted apart from his mother who was busy making ends meet with part-time jobs.

Years passed and the boy grew up resentful and estranged from his mother. He carried a void in his heart that was never filled. He blamed her for his problems. It was at this time that the boy met a girl, older and smarter than him, who returned his love. They decided to marry without asking for the blessings of the boy's mother, not considering it necessary. The woman did not fuss and reconciled in silence. She had already fallen into the habit of enduring whatever came her way.

It is now seven years since she moved in with them, and things that were on a downward spiral have now touched the nadir. Her isolation is complete with the son ensconced in his wife's arms and both husband and wife doting exclusively on their children and having no time for her. They made a life of their own within their nuclear family, separate from the woman. No one notices except for the woman. The estranged son has recovered his long-lost haven in his new family.

One day in the park she sees a man standing alone, distractedly crushing dried leaves under his shoes. Suddenly he turns and they look at each other. The man smiles hesitatingly, uncertain of her response. She is taken aback and her lean body trembles. There is a glint of keen curiosity in his eyes, an endearing softness that she finds irresistible. They shake hands and sit down on the worn-out wooden bench. As they converse empathy flows between them, an electric feeling of being lifelong friends. She feels the positive energy, sensing a strange and instant camaraderie. She has not felt this way for a long time. In these fleeting moments, their torched lives gush to embrace each other. She knows she has finally found a friend to fill the long, lonely hours, and instinctively knows he feels the same way. Their need is mutual and urgent. They are two beings yearning to escape their grinding life and have nothing to lose.

THE SABZWARIS

'Mother,' shouted Laila, 'the Sabzwaris' cat has overturned all the milk bottles in the doorway, again! Why don't you complain to them?'

Mother replied gently, 'Darling, I did a couple of times but they ignored me. They live in their own shell and I have decided to let the matter rest.'

Laila was surprised. 'Mother, they are a strange lot, quite an enigma to me.'

'Yes, they are! I think the time has come to tell you the story of the Sabzwari family. Now you must listen very attentively, dear.' Laila huddled up close to her mother and listened carefully as she narrated the story.

'My dear, life for the Sabzwaris was very different from what you see today. They were an affluent family with plenty of money and resources. They were people of repute and had links with those in the upper echelons of society. Mr Sabzwari owned a ginning factory and wielded strict control over his workers. He was a ruthless stickler for discipline and ran his business with a strict hand. His employees at the factory were scared of him. They were severely punished in case of any wrongdoing or dereliction of duty. It was known that few employees lasted for any length of time in this tense environment.

'The only person who stood up to Mr Sabzwari was Mrs Sabzwari. She was a tall, broad woman, in stark contrast to her husband's short and portly physique. Mr Sabzwari avoided confrontation with his wife, and when squabbles did erupt he ended them as quickly as he could. Many times he was heard saying with a heartfelt sigh, "It is no use arguing with women, they never listen to anybody." To which his stout wife would declaim, "As if you have the wisdom of the whole world incorporated in your thick head!" She would tower over him, her arms folded, scowling at him in an intimidating fashion. Mr Sabzwari looked at her helplessly, muttering under his breath, "Oh God, have mercy on me!" She belonged to a wealthy family, spoilt by too much attention and was too officious for his liking.

'The three children the Sabzwaris bore were a different breed from their parents. They were completely devoted to their parents, being the epitome of docility. Sometimes Mr Sabzwari would take them to the factory where they sat meekly, holding each other's hands, not daring to stray from their seats. They quietly watched their father curse and shout, creating order from disorder, and even disorder from order. The three talked in whispers amongst themselves, not daring to raise their voices. The employees watched the docile children with a mixture of alarm and amusement. They looked the opposite of their father. On their visits the children were routinely served orange juice, which they sipped slowly and cautiously. This was the closest they got to their father. Otherwise he kept his distance from them and was often heard saying, "Never question your elders, it is sheer insolence," raising his stubby finger at them and silencing them before they could speak. I heard that Mr Sabzwari's father was also very strict with him, and it was known that he was regularly flogged. However, Mr Sabzwari did no such thing to his children; he never applied the rod to them, having felt the damage it did to young minds. He was proud of his children, who were all models of compliant youth. Feroze, the eldest son, grew into a tall, lanky youth, with delicate features and gentlemanly ways. Safroze and Sita were blossoming into young, well-groomed-women.'

Mother now paused a while and took a deep breath, 'Now, listen carefully child: then something unbelievably tragic happened that changed the course of their lives forever.' Laila snuggled up closer to her mother, all ears, attentive.

'It was a horrific, tragic incident that shook everybody's lives, including ours. Mr and Mrs Sabzwari were shot in a grisly fashion during the riots that broke out in the factory. There was a collision with the labour union who demanded higher salaries and decent working hours. Mr Sabzwari had, as usual, been stubborn and refused to relent. One evening when the couple was driving to the factory to check on the workers a mob surrounded their car, brought it to a standstill and fired gunshots at them at close range. The bodies of the couple were riddled with bullets and they died on the spot. Later the men responsible for the killings were convicted and given the death sentence.

'The three children were stunned and in shock. When the coffins of the parents were carried to their final resting place they wailed helplessly, "How will we live without our beloved parents?" Feroze was as devastated as his sisters were, but remained stoic and struggled to console them. "Please don't cry, Mummy and Daddy would not like it.

They would want us to be strong." But it was tough on all of them to lose both parents simultaneously. Feroze had always been his mother's darling boy, hanging around her, running errands for her, and driving her to visit family and friends. Sometimes, in an indulgent mood, she would bake his favourite cookies and cakes. She came to rely more on him as he grew older, seeking his counsel when things went astray. Those days Mr Sabzwari was too immersed in his work and had turned into a workaholic. Mrs Sabzwari trusted her son the way she trusted nobody else, not even her husband. As for Feroze, his mother was the only woman he truly loved.

'The three siblings' ivory tower crumbled with the death of their parents. Having led a strictly sheltered life, they were ill-prepared to pick up the scattered pieces of their lives. Their routines had been regimented so they continued to follow the same pattern that they had lived when their parents were alive. With little experience, Feroze could not manage the family business that had been dominated by Mr Sabzwari who trusted nobody but himself. The lower management was not in his control and had turned intractable. Feroze barely visited the factory and delegated the task to employees who skimmed off all profits. Very soon the business was running at a loss and they filed for bankruptcy. With time, there was very little money in the coffers, and before long they were living off their savings that had been left by their rich and frugal parents.'

As Laila attentively listened, Mother said sadly, 'All those years we had known them well and were witness to their gradual decline. It is a very sad state of affairs when families lose everything and go downhill.'

Mother continued, 'The three siblings faithfully kept their parents' memories alive. They put up their photos on the walls and preserved their personal belongings. Nothing was discarded or moved and everything was kept meticulously in its own place. With time, the house became a museum, filled with a stale musty odour of old, disused relics. The lives of these three became equally mundane, boring and repetitive. The girls cooked, washed and did the housework the whole day whilst Feroze stood as a watchdog over them.

'One year after their parents' death, Feroze announced to his sisters that he would never marry and that he would always protect them in the way their parents had desired. He declared that allegiance to their parents' values and ethics would be their only goal in life. They all took a silent pledge and vowed to remain united through thick and thin.

'Then an incident happened that I learnt about through the grapevine years later. Sita, who had remained a restless, nonconforming soul, announced she was in love with Afridi, a young man who was a frequent visitor to their house. He was a tall, handsome boy with an amiable, somewhat ingratiating smile. Feroze had never really liked him but had still allowed him to visit them. He was always more interested in the girls and this mortified him. Then Sita threw the bombshell that Afridi had proposed to her! Feroze and Safroze were beside themselves with rage. Feroze shouted and cursed, and Safroze chided her loudly. Feroze remained unrelenting and declared that their parents would never have approved of that middle-class boy and so they could not give their consent.

'The matter did not end there. We heard through the neighbourhood grapevine that Afridi convinced Sita to elope with him, which she did. Feroze and Safroze were understandably shocked to discover Sita had run away, however, they didn't dare report the matter to the police, fearful of the disgrace it would bring the family. The brother and sister waited anxiously for several days but did not breathe a word to anyone. And then one day Sita returned, looking disheveled and distraught. She confessed that Afridi had abandoned her when his family forbade him from marrying her and, faced with their outrage, had insisted Sita return to her family. The brother and sister, angry and ashamed though they were, decided to put everything behind them. They hugged their sister and assured her that she was forgiven. The incident remained a secret between them.

'Life resumed as normal, Sita remained subdued and quiet, silently licking her wounds. Only Safroze livened up the atmosphere of the quiet house with her animated chatter on current affairs and family gossip. She was vivacious and the lively sound of her voice floated through the house. Safroze had stepped into her mother's shoes and took on her role in the household. She became motherly and was extra attentive to her siblings' needs. She cooked delicious meals daily. She loved animals and kept many cats, feeding them with great care and love. Like Feroze, Safroze had never considered marriage and now inwardly jeered her foolish sister who had eloped and had been shamefully jilted. Her sister's experience reinforced her belief that no man deserved to marry her. Men, she thought, were all a bunch of buffoons who used women and when they had had enough, discarded them.

'With time Safroze and Sita aged, but not gracefully. They stumbled into middle age, their faces smudged and faded. Even Safroze's animated chatter subsided over time. Feroze's bones had shrunk, his frame looked haggard and he slouched like a defeated man. His commitment to his sisters was absolute and gave meaning to his otherwise destitute existence.

'Every morning the three siblings drove their rusty, dusty car to a particular destination where their memories resided. They had picnicked here on weekends with their parents, far from the din of city life. Their past became alive here, memories swarmed in and their mood would lighten.'

Now her mother's voice waned as she reached the end of the story. Laila had not stirred throughout the long narrative. It was a strange, poignant story. As she looked out towards the house, the ghosts of the older Sabzwaris seemed to float in every room. It was clear that the legacy of their parents had been eternalised in the minds of their children, more so than it would have been had they lived.

THE STRANGER

A man and a woman sat in a club. They sat next to each other, primarily to interact closely, but they did not sit face to face. Thus, wary of intimacy, they created an unspoken distance, which suited both of them because of their sense of propriety.

The woman was pretty and fair complexioned with large, melancholy eyes. She was heavily made up, with her half-pouting full lips sending soft signals to her male companion. The man was well-groomed, wearing a crisp white *shalwar kameez*. He looked like a man of authority with a reputation to protect. He had a white, well-trimmed beard that covered half his face. He had small piercing eyes under thick, bushy brows.

A stranger observing them would not be able to gauge whether their relationship was sexual or plutonic. On closer observation it appeared to be sexual. They were not man and wife, for there was a certain stiffness in their demeanour, as if there were certain boundaries that could not be crossed between them. There was little chemistry between the two, yet they bonded as if satisfying a mutual need. In age they were far apart, the man being beyond middle age and she having barely entered that bracket.

The man was attentive to her, yet his discourse revolved around his children, as he proudly boasted of their achievements which he felt were akin to his own. 'My son graduates from Harvard University this year. He has always excelled in his studies. He has great potential and will go far in life. It was I who pushed him, motivated him and brought him to this stage.' Whilst he spoke he swelled his bosom and held his body erect. The woman listened, neither with too much attention nor with apathy, but looking unblinkingly at the man all the while. She seemed not to mind being at the receiving end of all this for it was nothing unusual for her. She was used to listening. He continued with his monologue as he had much to communicate, whilst she was content just to listen. Her voice was habitually subdued. The man ranted on about the turmoil in the country. 'It is all a mess and there is no one with good intentions who will clean it up. They are all stakeholders. We, the denizens of the state, have a responsibility but our hands are tied.' He lowered his voice and looked warily around. 'There are large conspiracies afloat, plots are being hatched externally to annihilate us. Foreign powers are hell bent against us.' She refrained from contradicting because she did not know enough to comment.

There was a commotion at the other end of the hall. The man rose to see what was happening. Loud voices filled the otherwise quiet hall. He was a man of action and authority and had to be in control. He walked over and talked to the men in a low but firm voice, calming them down. The voices subsided and the men reluctantly dispersed. He returned to the table where the woman was sitting patiently, like one used to enduring every kind of situation. She was rubbing her hands and it seemed like she was wanting to brush aside something that was on her mind. She asked, 'What was the commotion about?'

He answered with a wave of his hand, 'Oh, a member was

complaining about an inflated bill. The matter is resolved; it was a misunderstanding. The waiters, after all, are human, and mistakes can be made.'

They picked up their conversation from where they had left off, but the steam had fizzled out. There was a lapse during which they sat with their eyes averted. He wanted to reinvigorate the discourse. With sudden urgency in his voice, he addressed her, 'You have never discussed your children! Why?' She turned in her seat, as if she wanted to convey something, but something stopped her. She was wrestling with her inner demons.

Finally, she spoke, 'You know there is a confession I have to make today, which, if I deny myself, will suffocate me to death. I am a murderess! I killed my own child.'

He looked startled and half rose in great agitation, then sat back again. She continued, 'It was a traumatic miscarriage. I wanted the child badly but my husband didn't. He detested children, declared they would be an albatross around his neck. He even said they would steal my attention from him. In desperation, I aborted the child.' She was weeping softly and the tears rolled down her cheeks as she wiped them away. Now that she had thrown open the floodgates of her mind, there was no holding back, and she continued, 'He is a loveless man and the only person he has ever loved is himself. He breeds misery on himself and those around him, silently like a virus. Look at us two today! We are in tatters, body and spirit, living on separate islands.' Tears welled up in her eyes again and she brushed them away.

Then she got up suddenly and self-consciously as if ashamed of revealing too much. Reluctantly he rose too, not to close the episode of the day, but to continue it later. They decided to let things be for the present. This was apparently not a one-day affair, this had more substance in it, a measured longing to share each other's unknown pasts. Both were locked together in a strange intimacy which was primal and impetuous. As they took leave of each other, they promised to meet again.

That night when the woman reached home her husband was waiting for her. He did not look at her or speak to her and it was almost as if she did not exist. His sullen expression said it all. He usually didn't keep things to himself but that night he was quiet. This made her fearful of him, for he was a strange, elusive man who lacked self-control. In the mirror she saw her face and was dismayed to see it look so sickly, now that the deceptive make-up had been wiped clean. As she looked at her reflection, she saw two weary eyes looking back at her.

The next morning the sunshine slanted through the bedroom windows and the room remained still and quiet. Strangely the woman never woke up, for she was dead, apparently having died in her sleep. She lay there quietly, with her hands folded across her bosom, as if she was patiently enduring her lot. She died without having been afflicted by disease, or perhaps some insidious malaise had spread quietly through her body to assuage her loneliness. Or perhaps there had been a cruel intervention through another, between God's will and hers. Her death did not have a name or code. Her husband wept inconsolably. Now he was not in control, for the only woman he had always controlled was gone.

The people at the funeral discreetly kept a hushed silence. One of them was the bearded man who maintained a cautious distance from the husband. They did not speak to each other, though they were no strangers to one another. But he was a stranger to all the others present, and his face was ashen. He did not even know whether he belonged there or not, or whether he should have come at all. That morning, after hearing the news of her death, he had faltered many times, but then could not resist going. He wanted to see that beautiful, melancholy face one last time. He stared at her now, taking it all in. Then abruptly and silently, he left the room without a backward glance. Nobody noticed his exit except the husband, who then continued with the funeral proceedings.

THE TRIO

Sanaullah reclined in a wicker chair on the upper terrace, his lean legs outstretched, engrossed in reading the daily newspaper. A satisfied expression lit his robust but deeply lined face that revealed distinct signs of aging. Suddenly he raised his head irritably at the disturbance around him.

It was Halima, his sister, who was desultorily dusting the wicker chairs and humming in a low tone. 'Must you make this racket while I'm reading the newspaper?' Sanaullah complained irritably, 'It distracts me from my reading. Our astute journalist, Hashmi, was on the point of unfurling a conspiracy theory on the mastermind of a terror plot. And there you go snapping its thread off!'

Halima, keeping a stoic silence, put the duster aside and went and sat on one of the wicker chairs. Her older brother annoyed her, but she knew that being the man of the house, he was unduly privileged. After all, she and her younger sister, Sakina, were dependent on him. He managed the finances, paid the bills and performed the miscellaneous tedious jobs indispensable to running a house. He was a retired man, living off investments from good times, when prices of property were affordable. The security of the two women depended on him. A life without his protection would be akin to living in fear and uncertainty. In despair, they had to put up with his irascibility, like having to swallow a toxic and scalding potion.

In recent years Halima had begun to fear him. He had turned overbearing and self-centered, and not the compassionate brother she had once known. It was age that made him cranky as he habitually berated them. 'Can't you two do something better for yourselves? Your untidy habits disgust me! The house is always in a mess!' The sisters, sick to the bones of daily housekeeping chores, would listen in silence.

Sanaullah flung the newspaper aside, his face contorted with anger. He scowled at Sakina who had quietly appeared. 'Where is my morning tea? I can see you two are getting lazy, you need a push and shove from me.' Sakina, timid as a mouse, scurried to the kitchen where the kettle was whistling loudly. She returned within minutes with a mug of steaming hot tea.

Sanaullah took it without a word of thanks, his eyes brooding and narrow as he drank the sugary, strongly brewed tea. He looked complacent, a man who lauded himself on being the epitome of wisdom and goodness, who shouldered the burden of two spinster sisters. If it wasn't for these cursed sisters, he would have enjoyed conjugal bliss and been a true lord of the manor. He remembered his mother's words, 'Promise me son, you will always take care of your sisters.' He had sacrificed his life just to keep their body and soul intact, and couldn't hold back his resentment. Many pretty girls had pursued him in his heyday and he prided himself on being an eligible bachelor, handsome and of no meagre means. He lacked nothing, but fate and providence were not aligned with him.

Having drunk his tea, he got up slowly and walked over to his bedroom. He bathed and dressed carefully, a man with a mission. He stared at himself in the mirror as he combed his thinning hair, half-wishing he had a wig to camouflage his age. He sprayed on strong cologne and sauntered out of the bedroom, locking the door behind him. He slipped out of the house and swiftly drove his shining new Suzuki out of the metal gate.

When his car disappeared around the corner the two sisters began complaining in high-pitched tones. Halima remarked sarcastically, 'He acts like the lord of a manor.'

Sakina moaned, 'And here we are, doing all the drudgery. It isn't fair! It just isn't fair!'

Halima loudly mouthed a list of complaints, 'He gives us a paltry sum of money to spend, barely enough to dress ourselves, and here we are, sitting in our old rags, whilst he dresses himself in fashionable new clothes.'

Sakina returned to the kitchen to prepare the day's meal as was her custom. She finally emerged looking tired and slovenly, her white hair tangled and unkempt. She slumped on a small stool on the terrace sipping a mug of steaming tea. Her glazed eyes stared into empty space as she picked her long, wiry hair, fitfully and distractedly.

Her gaze now alighted on her sister, lounging in the wicker chair idly going through a fashion magazine. An uncontrollable anger erupted in Sakina. She picked up her empty cup and flung it like a missile towards her sister. They say that witches gain extra muscle in a paroxysm of rage. Halima ducked quickly but not before the mug struck her chin, cutting her skin open and drawing blood. Sakina, in that moment, cowered in fear, expecting a backlash. As abruptly as she had lashed out, she was overtaken by remorse and rushed to fetch a swathe of bandages and cleaned her sister's wound. 'Forgive me, Halima, I think I lost my mind.' Halima was in shock and could not believe that her docile sister could be capable of such rage and violence. She felt sorry for herself and loathed her sister.

Later in the day Sanaullah returned, looking sleek and smug. He nodded at his sisters, looking them over as if they were pieces of old furniture, redundant but secure, and walked tiredly towards his room.

'Should I lay out the food for you?' Sakina obligingly asked.

His response was a curt reply, 'Don't bother! I have eaten.' With this he shut the door, but not before a dense waft of perfume sailed into the room.

The two women puckered their faces, exchanging knowing looks. They suspected the reason for their brother's escapades, but uttered not a word of disapproval. It was a man's privilege, they had known and heard. What else could a bachelor do, if he didn't negotiate his way through a solitary situation? They knew the biological needs of men, much as they knew about men's skills at keeping their womenfolk harnessed.

Sanaullah was riding on a high horse these days. His lonely hours were spent in the company of a very beautiful woman. She was fair complexioned with delicate features, combined with a sharp intellect and wit. Sanaullah's head was in the clouds, having accomplished a heroic feat of winning this lovely lady's heart. He was a savvy man, somewhat delusional, and was convinced that women found him to be irresistible. He bragged endlessly, 'When I was in college, I was a Casanova, and girls buzzed around me like bees, but I distanced myself from them all.' The woman listened to him passively, she had no reason to disbelieve him.

Their courtship continued with undiminished passion, but it was a flagging ship with nowhere to go. She was an unattached woman, although in her youth she had had a stream of suitors. She had married a man of great wealth but she had borne him no children. Then he died suddenly and she enjoyed his great fortune. In her later age she was lonely, desperately needing a man to fill her empty days. She had met Sanaullah at a party and the two were instantly attracted to each other. Their desire and need for each other was mutual. Since then he constantly sought her company and his visits to her house became more frequent.

Their aging bodies fed off each other, like long-lost lovers, both insatiate. And there was always a small ring, or a necklace, or a bracelet to adorn her body that he quietly slipped on her before he would leave. 'Beautiful! I just love it!' She would murmur in his ears, as she twitched his hairy ear lobes between her slender fingers. Those words, uttered in a quivering, tremulous voice, were all he wanted to hear. His aging heart soaked them up greedily. She knew well the art of seduction, 'You are such a handsome man!' she would repeatedly tell him. 'You are better than all the younger men. Perhaps this is the reason you make me feel young.'

He was jubilant and kissed her. 'I like the way you dress – it's very becoming for your age, unlike other fashion-addicted women. You have class and elegance. I don't like crass women who always have a motive lurking somewhere.' Together they lived out their dreams in these intimate moments.

The two sisters did not resemble each other, even remotely. Halima was tall, painfully emaciated, a dried-up bamboo, with straight, stringy white hair brushing her lean shoulders. With the years catching up with her, she walked unsteadily, struggling to balance her body, but she retained her spirit. In comparison, Sakina was a diminutive woman with hunched shoulders - a posture that added years to her age. Age had also shrunk her body, giving her a look of compressed baggage. Over the years her personality had been strangled by her loneliness and a life without meaning.

Halima possessed greater gumption than her sister, having learnt early to negotiate on her own terms without fear of being bulldozed. In her younger days she had been obsessed with men, but most of them were not good enough for her. She had once fallen in love but the man was cold and unresponsive. His interest was elsewhere. She was devastated and didn't ever want to risk getting hurt again. She made a pact with herself never to get involved with a man again. Her trust in men never recovered and she grew resigned to a life as a single person. Life compensated her in other ways. She possessed the flair of a social butterfly and was popular amongst her group of friends.

The sisters clashed together like old brass cooking pots. Sakina blamed her sister for her trials. A quiet mousy woman, she was generous to a fault. She was the one to perform the arduous chores of cooking and cleaning the house, while her two siblings, perched on their self-anointed thrones, hardly moved. The least she expected from them was gratitude. Their haughty and overbearing attitude suggested otherwise. Halima belittled her mercilessly, 'You are an anti-social woman and I can prove it! You have no friends and you never will!' Such cruel words unhinged Sakina and she shrank into her small world. Hers was a fantasyland that was her comfort zone where she retreated when times were rough. Her siblings, accustomed to her eccentricities, ignored her. Her dreams took on a life of their own. She began to hallucinate wildly and told her sister in sinister tones, 'The trees in our garden talk at nightfall, I can hear them. It is the wailing of a demon. Yesterday I saw the ghost of our dead mother, and she beckoned me to her with her wide open arms.'

Halima had started frequently lashing out in anger at her sister, unaware of the how deeply she hurt her. With time, Sakina became quieter and withdrew into a dark shell, going around the house with a dark morose look on her face. She shut herself in her room for hours at a time and morphed into a living ghost. The three siblings were all living in their own dark world, the space between them was getting more desolate, but they were too engrossed in their own situations to notice it.

Finally, one day Sakina disappeared. No one noticed her absence until the evening, when dinner was not served as usual. 'Where is Sakina?' roared Sanaullah, his appetite flaring up.

Halima rushed into the kitchen in consternation, 'Oh where has that woman disappeared? She did not have the decency to inform me where she was going.'

'Is this not an unearthly hour for a woman to be out of the house?' fumed Sanaullah. 'I will beat her sore when she returns!'

Night deepened into blackness and yet there was no sign of Sakina. They enquired from the neighbours, but no one had seen her that day. They drove around the neighbourhood, hoping to see her on the dimly lit roads, but there was no sign of her. Sakina had disappeared into thin air!

They spent the night in great anxiety, with Sanaullah pacing up and down, Halima prostrated herself in prayer. Sanaullah informed the police, giving a detailed description of his missing sister.

The night slipped by and still no sign of her. Outside the cold winter air roared and sleet descended on the land carpeting it with white slush. The house within was deathly silent and an eerie gloom descended. Brother and sister looked at each other, a spectre of fear loomed. For the first time in years they sorely missed their sister. They missed her pinched self-effacing face, habitually quiet like a mouse, but with the alacrity of a pounding hare when she had chores to perform. The food lay cold and untouched on the table, for neither had the appetite to eat a morsel. Perhaps they could not because Sakina was not there to heat it for them.

The phone rang, loud and eerie in the dark, and Sanaullah jumped out of his chair where he had spent the night, not having slept a wink. All night he had brooded and lamented, questioning why things had come to this pass when he was a good man and had done well by his sisters. It was the police, 'Sir, come immediately to the Rose Garden. Our man has just spotted a lady there who matches your description of your sister. She is in a state of stupor.'

Within a matter of minutes, the two reached the park. Two policemen stood there, waiting. In a corner of the park, on a wooden bench, crouched Sakina, like a curled cat. Her back was turned to them. Her hair looked whiter than ever covered with sleet.

'Sakina!' they called out together in one trembling voice. The woman did not stir. With their hearts pounding they rushed forward, shouting again, 'Sakina! Sakina!' Halima grasped her shoulder and shook it violently. It was icy cold. At her touch Sakina's body slumped to one side like a rag doll. Her face was white and frozen and two glassy eyeballs stared out at them. They let out a terrified scream that echoed loudly in the still air.

For a long time only a low wailing sound was heard, interspersed with anguished sobs, as brother and sister collapsed on the wet ground.

Halima was left alone to handle the ire of Sanaullah who would soon forget his dutiful and docile sister Sakina when he was in the arms of his beautiful mistress.

THE END

WE LIVE IN STRANGE TIMES

Two men sat under a banyan tree. Twilight was descending. Overhead, vultures hovered with intent, in

huge clusters, darkening a pale sky.

'We live in strange times.'

Said one man to the other.

'The pestilence has sucked our bone marrow

Brought out a two-legged paradox in our lives'

'What may that be?'

The other man asked.

'The plight of the opposites,

The rich are more miserable, more fearful today,

having acquired too much,

whereas the poor are more carefree

having little to lose or gain.'

The man who spoke first, continued,

'He that is educated, polished, has as few defenses

as the illiterate man, if not less, against fear,

The educated mind has capacity for more terror, fear,

than the illiterate man, whose mind has too little imagination

to soak in much suffering and fear.'
The other man acquiesced,
'Yes, strange times call for strange revelations.'

The first man spoke again,
'Fear is more powerful and lethal
than death itself,
for in my fragility, in my fear,
there is more to be endured,
more pain and grief than I can bear
than in my death.'

And then the man continued,
'Loneliness is fraught with fear
It piles up like sediment on the bedrock of a river
And then starves the spirit.'

The first man spoke again
'Our worst enemy is ourselves, be on guard against Self,
For our capacity to destroy ourselves be as compelling
As our capacity to destroy others.
That is why empires fall and crumble
Like a house of cards.'
The other man acquiesced in silence.

The first man spoke again.

'We are intimidated, in awe of the big things, the larger picture,

whereas it is the smaller things (like the virus) that has the power to destroy.

Comrade, I forewarn you

When I say, never underestimate the power of the underdog

Or the man on the leash.'

As the darkness around them deepened they knew it was time to leave. Together they rose and slowly walked out of the dark night.

IN THE WORST OF TIMES

In the palatial house where luxury and opulence, rather than human beings, wore an emblem of greatness, was located in a posh locality in the capital. These affluent people, the elite of the country, enjoyed every amenity that money could buy, the best food, the ideal holiday in foreign countries, the highest accolades, just by wishing it to happen. They had a magic wand in their hands, and their wish was instantly granted. They were like spoilt, gifted children, who were never wanting in life's beneficence.

Then a pestilence fell from the skies like a thunderbolt, and their lives took an uneasy somersault, their peace, harmony and joys extinct in a moment. The inmates of this house, a couple, Iqbal and Samina, and their two children, reacted instantly. They were educated, polished, worldly-wise, knew the ramifications of the disease. They isolated themselves completely in the house, announced firmly in their social circles that they were not open to visitors. Half of the domestic servants, twenty in number, were given paid leave to go to their villages and not return till things were back to normal. The delighted servants joyfully went home to make merry with their families, mindless of the monster disease growing in their midst. The ones who were permitted to stay, were those who were indispensable, without whom the smooth orderliness of the house would collapse, and create greater misery for the employers. However, they were ordered strictly to follow a regimen of maintaining distance, hourly handwashing and disinfecting themselves, although these held no meaning for them, yet in their enslaved situations, they could not refuse.

Fear continued to stalk the house, like an apparition, that was invisible, yet stamped its foot everywhere. Fear was filtered down to the children from the parents, and they went around with subdued faces. Fear became a fixture in the minds of the parents, who were, besides other things, in a vulnerable age bracket. For once life was not in their control, money ceased to be monolithic, could not shield them. They were as helpless, fragile, as their domestic servants and all the poor, who infested the country. Disease was a leveler, reduced them all to the lowest denominator, and they were utterly defenseless. The pandemic spared no one, and death became a number to be counted daily in the crowded cemeteries all over the world.

Then news of the death of Iqbal's parents had reached them, adding to their afflictions. They died a week after one another. The family was devastated, as Iqbal wept, 'They were healthy both of them, and now gone in a matter of weeks. I will never forgive myself for not saying my last farewell to them and attending the final rites. They were totally undemanding in both life and death. This virus is brutal, callous and ruthless.'

Henceforth, the family, became more cloistered, more isolated. Fear mixed with grief, had made zombies out of them, as daily they remained glued to television and mobile phones. The elders listened to the news broadcasts, relaying the daily death toll in millions. The youngsters needed to escape, and were hooked to video chats and games. They became lethargic and developed a growing addiction to snacks, administered to them hourly by the domestic servants. Everybody's life was on hold, cut down to the miniscule, fragmentary basics.

One day, a domestic servant developed a fever and a wheezing cough. Iqbal told his wife that he had caught the virus, and in fear of infection, they packed him off to his village. Samina was relieved, 'Thank God, he is gone, but he could have infected us already.' Anxiety in the house grew as the space for its breeding grew more expansive.

The following night, a police squad raided their house, and demanded to see the domestic servant who had caught the virus. 'We sent him to his village,' Iqbal told the man.

'Do you not know you were supposed to inform the hospital. This man will infect the whole village. You have committed a crime by violating the law, it is such as you that we have to control now. You are under arrest.' The constable was frothing with rage.

Consequently, Iqbal was arrested, and spent a night in jail. The next day when he returned home, having bribed the constable, he was a broken, man. ‘I have never known such humiliation in my entire life. How dare they do this to me. I shall see to it, that the men are punished.’

And then when he launched a complaint, nothing happened. They knew time was not on their side now. They felt betrayed. Who says the pandemic is not a leveler?

THE GREAT CONTAGION

In Nature's realm:
It is springtime
Gardens bloom with colorful flora
Roses blush blood red, black,
Brutally seductive
Magnolias cavort in the breeze
swirling like lover to the beloved
Animals sprint in sheer abandonment
Birds leisurely glide in azure skies.
The air is pure, cleansed
In purgatorial frenzy.
The planet breathes a sigh of relief
After its dizzy spree of busyness

Today, for all humanity:
Darkness seals gloom everywhere,
Around us, below us, above us,
A shroud of death envelops,
Millions struggle for life, die alone,
Crave for a human touch,
They die, fearful, devastated, solitary,
Today neither flowers, nor funeral ceremonies,

will celebrate,
their lifetime of loving deeds
their sacrifice, honor, struggle
joy, tireless pain and fidelity
endured, through a life-span

In the morgues
The dead pile up
The wait is too long
The cemeteries too crowded.

Today millions in quarantine, self-isolated,
Hunger for human bonding, for the other
Dense, bustling, cities, lie silent, deserted,
In fear of the Contagion
Where carnivals were endlessly played
Bars, theatres, overflowed with spectators,
Cities that never slept, never paused to think,
Today are at a stand-still,
Like tombs of a lost civilization,
Long vanquished by natural forces.

There are no weapons of defense
to fight the virulent virus

scurrying through every corner of the globe
hitching itself to petrified victims
groveling, in utter dismay

The apocalypse strikes
At the roots of human life-line
And, in a fraction, plunges races, nations,
Reeling on a death-riven threshold,
As the earth rocks perilously
Between life and death
Perforce, humanity, stands together
In its existential survival
Multitudes choking on their last breath
Pleading to their Saviour, to salvage them
From the fangs of the Contagion,
And heal the deepening wounds.